Claws Out

by

Evadeen Brickwood

Episode 2

Charlie Proudfoot would rather not get involved in solving murders, but her friend Lerato Gwala, a private detective from Johannesburg, believes that Charlie's talent of intuition will give her murder investigations the edge. So Charlie agrees to help Lerato with just one more case.

In this Episode:

Scientists are working with endangered African wild dogs in the Kruger Park. But not everyone in their camp seems to have the same priorities.

When Professor Gerald Morton does not return from a drive to observe a pack of dogs, the members of his project team are soon making a grisly discovery.

Why would anyone try to sabotage their research and what does the professor's ex-wife know about his murder?

<u>Other Titles by Evadeen Brickwood</u>

In the time travel youth series:

"Children of the Moon" ("Remember the Future 1")

in the German Edition:

"Kinder des Mondes" ("Erinnerung an die Zukunft 1")

"The Speaking Stone of Caradoc" ("Remember the Future 2")

"The Secret of the Bird God" ("Remember the Future 3")

Novels:

"A Half Moon Adventure" (An Adventure Mystery)

"Abenteuer Halbmond" (German Edition)

"Singing Lizards" (A Mystery-Adventure set in Africa)

"Singende Eidechsen" (German edition)

"The Rhino Whisperer" (A Crime Mystery)

"Der Nashorn Flüsterer" (German edition)

Other Titles by Evadeen Brickwood

In the Charlie Proudfoot series so far:

1) A Hazy Shade of Murder

Special Thanks and Acknowledgements

Many thanks to my many beta readers for their constructive editing and proofreading efforts. Geoff Mulder and Svenja Bottner for their efforts in helping design the unique book covers. SanParks rangers and all organisations and volunteers, who tirelessly strive for the conservation of wild species such as the African wild dog.

For Gerald

Chapter ONE

Professor Gerald Morton flung his khaki sunhat onto the seat next to him and let the afternoon wind rush through his thinning hair. The breeze carried the dusty smell of the savannah and made his shirt flutter as he steered the open jeep along a bumpy dirt road in the Kruger National Park. He was on his way to a pack of wild dogs he had been monitoring, to collect some last data that would assist his team with their conservation efforts.

Gerald Morton was the head of the research team and he thoroughly enjoyed the last moments of solitude in the park. Tomorrow, they would wrap things up at the camp, and as so often, he dreaded having to return to the city.

Over the past 10 days, they had worked their way from the northern-most dens of the wild dogs down to Phalaborwa and Tamboti. The scientists were particularly interested in the denning habits of the endangered animals after the rare event of welcoming new pups to the packs.

During the denning season, they frequently changed their burrows. Wild dogs did this to get other predators off their trail or to escape fleas and parasites at the old place. The pack close to Tamboti had no intentions of making detection easy, so the team had scouted the area for a possible location. Now it was time to find the new den where the dogs had carried their 2-months-old offspring.

Tonight it was Thokozo's turn to prepare an edible dinner over the open fire with the last of the provisions they had brought with them. Dr. Thokozo Sibanda, a fellow zoologist at the prestigious university in Johannesburg, was not a half-bad cook and Gerald Morton had learned a few tricks from him over the years. The rest of the team consisted of a veterinarian, Dr. Nivedna Naidoo, Pericles Duncey, their only volunteer on this expedition, and a grade student by the name of Irina Lotcombe. Irina aided the senior scientists mostly with record keeping and putting tracking devices on the adult animals before they were released back into the wild.

The student shared a tent with Dr. Naidoo, who provided expert advice and treated occasional injuries. Last week, one of the dogs had been badly injured by a random snare and they'd organised a helicopter to the nearest vet clinic. Dr. Naidoo was a brash woman, but the two of them got on surprisingly well, considering the lack of space and privacy in the tent.

Sadly though, none of the women could cook. Since the nearest town was a long drive away, the men shared the task of making dinner.

Otherwise, they stuck to staples like cereal, minute noodles and long-life milk during the day. On the way from Johannesburg, it had been a tight squeeze in their off-road vehicles next to boxes with provisions, their equipment and canisters with water and petrol. Considering the limited funding for their research project, luxuries were out of the question, but Morton had forked out money to buy bags of macadamia nuts and oranges from a farm stall next to the road.

'I won't take long,' he had said to Thokozo Sibanda and packed the equipment into the back of the jeep. The antenna was basic and a bit awkward to handle, but the results were worth their efforts.

'No problem, Prof, just be back before nightfall. I'm sure the stew will be done by then.' Dr. Sibanda had kept stirring the pot over the fire pit because the gas cooker had given out days ago.

'Smells delicious.' Gerald Morton smiled. He had received some unexpected news that morning and was in a good mood.

'Must be the Maggi seasoning,' Dr. Sibanda had said and added chopped onions to the pot. 'I like cooking, but my wife won't let me into the kitchen at home. She says it's her domain.'

'Lucky you,' Prof Morton had replied. 'It would have been great if my ex-wife could cook. Maybe our marriage would have lasted.' They both knew the true reason for the divorce, however.

'Thin ice my man, thin ice…' Dr. Sibanda had chuckled. 'One might think you were a sexist pig. What's Jeanne up to these days? The botany project? Are you still waiting for the patent?"

'You know how long it takes for patents to come through. She's busy with some other study and probably a new lover for all I care.'

Prof Morton avoided a direct answer to his friend's

question. There would be more than enough time after their trip to talk about his exciting news. Right now, the wild dogs needed their undivided attention.

'Well, everyone to his own,' Thokozo Sibanda had mused and added some spices to his dish. He stirred and the aroma of cumin and coriander rose from the pot.

'Can't wait to have a taste of this.' Gerald Morton sniffed the air as he secured the antenna. Then he checked the petrol gauge and refilled his water bottle. All set.

His marriage had amazingly lasted for six years. It was the mistake of his life and they'd never had any children. He'd been content with their arrangement, despite Jeanne's many affairs, but she'd wanted her freedom in the end.

The divorce had been brief and painless as it should be between two educated people. No hard feelings. And now four years had gone by, so he was well and truly over it. Despite his good looks, Gerald Morton had no time for love. In any case, he had to channel his energies into more important matters right now. The Wild Dog Conservation Project being one of them.

Tomorrow, they would break camp and drive south to a guesthouse in Hoedspruit where they'd spend the night and make themselves presentable for civilisation again. With some luck, there would be electricity, enough hot water for all of them to shower, and a decent meal.

During their stay in the Kruger Park, Alan, one of the local rangers, who had family in Hoedspruit, was in constant contact with the team. He usually tipped them off about new developments. Alan had been certain that the pack in their current location was on the move. Probably due to a roaming leopard rather than a flea infestation, this time.

The town of Hoedspruit was a welcome halfway station between the bush and the city. Alas, they didn't have a choice. Professor Morton needed to prepare for a presentation to attract new donors. Wild dogs were not as exciting as, let's say, rhinos, elephants and lions, but since funding was crucial to their conservation project, the university had organised a cocktail event and a tour of the Kruger for the donors at the end of the month. The prospects were promising.

Irina, the grad student was putting together a

stunning presentation with photographs she had taken during the trip. If that didn't win over some well-funded organisations and the occasional philanthropist, then he didn't know what would. Irina was also halfway done with the report and his speech. He couldn't be bothered with all that computer stuff.

In April, he had spoken to Dr. Harold Carter at the International Conference for Wildlife Conservation in New York. Carter was coming to South Africa, and Josephine Murray from London was seriously considering her attendance, as were representatives of large corporations and banks. Hopefully, there would be more confirmations by the end of the week.

Perhaps the tide is turning, at last, Prof. Morton thought as he drove along the dirt road and negotiated a particularly sandy patch just before the road forked. He headed to the slope just above a wooded area, where the wild dogs had last been spotted.

Morton buttoned up his shirt, clipped pens into his breast pocket and took up his observation post just below the slope. The equipment was quickly set up in a tiny camouflaged tent and he began to monitor the adult dogs, holding up the antenna that tracked the signals.

Yup, no doubt about it: the pack was on the move.

He zoomed in and spotted a female with a broad black stripe on her back, tenderly carrying one of the pups in her jaws. The camera clicked away as she hurried towards a crack between piles of rocks on the other side of two fresh-water pools. He scribbled down his observations as the receiver beeped. The readings showed that the female was first-time mother Cindy.

"Got you, Cindy. Now, who is this adorable puppy you've got there?" He mumbled. "Looks like I was just in time."

They hadn't even named the fluffy pups yet, just Pup 1, 2, 3 and 4. When they grew older, they would receive proper names and collars.

There was no sign of the lone leopard that was making the pack jittery. Several wild dogs splashed around at the water's edge by the thicket. Denver and Toni, by the looks of it… and Harry, a male in his prime. Morton wondered how many pups they had already carried across.

Cindy disappeared into the new den, followed by Sophie, another bitch. The signal grew faint. Soon, she reappeared with Sophie and they headed back to the site of the old den. The trees were obstructing his view and Morton moved forward to get a better look. He studied the dogs' movements through his binoculars and was so engrossed in his work that he didn't watch his step. Not a good idea, as the ground was covered in loose rocks and the last rains had carved a step into the hard soil. If he could just get a bit closer…

His sturdy boot caught in the flat loop of a tree root that was firmly attached to the ground. He fell hard, twisting his ankle despite the protective boot. A blinding pain shot through his foot and the elbow that had broken his fall. The strap around his neck had somehow snapped and sent the binoculars flying.

"Oh great. Bloody, f***ing hell…" he shouted. "Damn stupid, f***ing…"

Cursing didn't help, of course, but it seemed to make the pain less noticeable as he began to pull his boot out from under the root. He crept towards the binoculars. They didn't seem damaged. Good.

He picked them up, knotted the strap around his neck and wiped the bloodied sand off his elbow before he loosened the bootlaces. Taking the footwear off was easier said than done. He moaned and pulled harder. His foot popped out of the boot. The sock hid a discoloured ankle, sore to the touch. For all he could tell, it wasn't broken, just sprained.

"Great!" He exclaimed. "God d***ed!"

Just his luck. What was he supposed to do now? Of course, the radio was in the jeep and calling for help was out of the question. He might spook the dogs and the chances that anybody would hear him were extraordinarily slim. So he rested his foot on the sturdy boot and waited. The pain subsided a little. Maybe he could manage to hop back to the shelter and deposit the binoculars there, then go up the slope somehow and contact the camp.

The sun was sinking fast and a faint sickle moon rose against the dark blue sky. There was a cold draft, and night-time in the bush meant all sorts of dangers.

That left him no choice. The Professor stood up, balancing the boot in his hand and began hopping the short distance to the tent. It would have been comical, had it not been for the pain.

Dammit, he thought, I should put ice on it or a bag of frozen peas. But he knew that none of the above was available even at their camp close to the Punda

Maria Gate. Morton wasn't too worried about leaving the equipment and notes behind. His colleagues could collect everything when they arrived, but would they find him anytime soon? Of course, they will, he thought and relaxed.

From the tent, it was still a good ways up the slope and after limping for a few minutes, he had to sit down. I should crawl back to the jeep, he thought. His ankle was swollen by now, so he couldn't put the boot back on his foot. He tied it by the laces to the back of his belt and began crawling up the path, ignoring the pain. Avoiding the sharp rocks wasn't easy in the dusk, but he did the best he could.

It grew darker and he heard loud yelping in the distance. Morton was startled and stopped for a moment. The dogs were surely in their new den by now, and the yelping sounded more like hyenas that were roaming close by. That's all he needed!

He had to make a better effort. It was safer to sit in the car and a whole lot more comfortable than here on the cold rocky ground. There was nothing but fabric to protect his knees against devil thorns and sharp stones but he kept crawling. "Ouch! Dammit!" He swore under his breath.

The stone had not cut through the robust fabric of his cargo pants, but the pain in his shin didn't make things any better.

Perhaps he should just grind his teeth and hop up the slope! He pushed himself up and hopped on one foot, steadying himself with his hands on the ground, his leg behind him in the air. Progress was slow, but at least there was progress.

As the light faded, the animal noises around him grew louder. A deep growl not far from the path made him jump. "Great, now the leopard is getting a whiff of me!" The academic said aloud as if the sound of his voice could ward off dangerous creatures.

"Dammit! Where are you guys? Come looking for me already!" The team knew more or less where he was, so why were they not coming? And what about Alan, the ranger? He moved closer to the vehicle and heard the radio crackling softly. 'Come in... come in...'

"I'm f***ing trying! F**k, that's sore!"

He lifted himself over the edge and sat down at the top of the slope, panting as if he'd just run a marathon. "Okay, back on your feet, soldier!" Now there were just a few meters left. The thought of resting on the car seat gave him his second wind, but before he managed to get up, a car approached on the main road and headed in his direction. Morton plopped back down with a sigh of relief and waved.

"Finally!" He grunted when he could see two bright cones cutting through swirling dust. In the dark, he couldn't make out, who was driving or how many people were sitting in the car.

It didn't matter, as long as somebody was coming to his rescue. Who else could it be but his colleagues? "Over here, I'm here!" He shouted and waved.

They must have seen the jeep and would be here within minutes. Professor Morton felt relieved. Now, that help had arrived, the scary animal sounds in the bush didn't worry him anymore.

The round headlamps grew larger as they bounced closer. The advancing vehicle came straight towards him, bobbing over sandy dips in a cloud of dust. He had to shield his eyes with his arm because the lights blinded him.

The car stopped close to the jeep he'd been trying to reach. Somebody in heavy boots got out and walked towards him, carrying an object. He assumed that it was a large torchlight or a gun to keep wild animals in check. The headlights still blinded him and he was unable to see, who his rescuer was.

"At last!" He cried. "Turn down the headlights, I can't see a thing! Had to leave everything down there when I hurt my foot. We should get it before we leave."

He turned around and pointed at the spot, where he had left the equipment in the little tent. It was odd that there was no greeting. Next thing he heard crunching steps behind him and he felt the impact of something heavy against the back of his head. Bright flashes danced before his eyes as he was flung forward by the blow and landed on his sore knees. This could NOT be true!

He'd been worried about wild animals and a cold night in the bush and now he was attacked by one of his colleagues! His own colleagues! Or maybe he had been wrong and it wasn't them at all. He tried to turn and look at his assailant.

"What on earth…"

The force of a second strike landed the professor on his stomach and he began to slide down the slope. His head was exploding with pain, then his eyesight ceased.

"Why?" He tried to scream. "Why are you doing this to me? Stop! STOP!"

But only a gurgling sound escaped his mouth as he tasted blood and sand.

There was nothing he could do to stop the brutal assault. Big and strong as he was, Gerald Morton had lost control of his sight and his voice. He couldn't move and there was nothing to be done.

WHY?! His mind kept screaming as he heard a voice calling from somewhere. Was it the radio in his car? It didn't matter now. Nothing mattered anymore. Anger, pain and betrayal; it all faded away. Faded, faded... He could no longer feel the next impact or the following one as he kept sliding head-down arms outstretched on the dusty, rocky slope.

Oddly, all he could think about was that now, he'd never get a taste of Thokozo's stew before his breathing ceased at the start of a peaceful night in the bush.

*

'I'm not sure I want to do this, Lerato,' Charlie Proudfoot moaned. 'How long has it been since we closed that last case of yours? Two months or so? Geez.'

It was already May and they were approaching winter. Her friend Lerato Gwala, the quick-witted private inspector, was on the other end of the line. Apparently, Lerato needed Charlie's help again with some new murder case that involved wild dog conservation.

Somebody had been murdered in the Kruger Park and clues were hard to come by, but just about the last thing on Charlie's mind was solving a murder case. She needed to find a job, needed to give her life purpose. The accident that had taken her husband and unborn child from her, lay more than two years in the past, and it was time for her to get her life back on track.

'Two and a half months. But what has that got to do with anything?'

'And then, what do I know about zoology or wild dogs? My field is genetics.'

'Who said you have to know anything about zoology or wild dogs? What do I know about that? All I need you to do is put your head around this case. The way you did before - easy peasy. And by the way, you probably know a lot more about zoology than I ever will, but it's your other talent I need. You didn't happen to have a dream about scientists or wild dogs or the Kruger Park, did you?'

'Are you still going on about my 'talent'? And no, I didn't even have a glimpse of wild dogs or the bush or murdered people. Nothing like that at all. And what do you mean by easy peasy? I'm not a human jukebox. Plop a coin in and I'll sing.' Charlie wanted to say a lot more but Lerato didn't seem to listen, as she was already filling her in on the case.

'The head of the faculty contacted me about an hour ago. The police are down to a wire. It was clearly no accident. The poor guy's head was bashed in... severe contusions to the back of the head. Murder weapon a heavy object ... the coroner's report says. This professor what's-his-name wants us to solve the murder of his colleague, another professor. He heard about our detective agency from a friend who'd followed the Deepak Misra case and how we handled it. And Andy thought it was a good idea to take the job.'

Andy Malherbe was Lerato's colleague from back in the day when they had both been employed by the Cape Town police department. Now they ran a fledgeling PI agency in Johannesburg.

'How did this 'head of the faculty' hear about us? They didn't even mention our names in the news.'

'I know, isn't that great. Word of mouth, that's what it is! He googled Maitirelo PI Agency and voilà, our website comes up.' Lerato was obviously excited.

'Good for you guys.'

'Actually, it was Andy's idea to ask for your help this time. Of course, we'll pay you again as a consultant. The police in those rural areas don't always seem to be on the ball when it comes to high-profile cases. Plus, the murder victim was cremated yesterday. So all we have are crime scene photographs, coroner's report and the first police report, including the witness statements.'

'Why was the murder victim cremated?'

'Religious reasons and nobody objected. Totally against procedure. We don't have much to go on. That's why the police commissioner wants outside consultants to assist them. We even have an inspector here in Joburg, who was assigned to us. Homicide's not so bad and we would be assisting each other. Your talent worked like a charm in Cape Town.'

'Yeah, and we nearly got pushed off a cliff and then those thugs shot at us in Cape Town when we were following the suspect… and what not. Great stuff.' Charlie rolled her eyes, but of course, Lerato couldn't see that.

'But we did it, didn't we?' Lerato tried to sound enthusiastic. 'We helped save an innocent woman.'

'Yes, we did, but let's see what the courts decide. Maybe they let him off the hook again. Proceedings like that can take a while."

"Well, we did what we could."

"Yep, but I thought it would be the last time that you needed my help.'

'Come on, Charlie, it's not as if you are busy right now,' Lerato said.

That was true. Charlie Proudfoot was still in the process of settling in and getting the house and garden into shape, but she didn't have a job. Be that as it may… she wasn't too keen on being dragged into yet another adventure involving crimes and especially murder.

'Why can't you and Andy work this case together? I'm yet to meet this mysterious partner of yours, who is so much better qualified to solve cases than I am.'

'I know. I have to introduce the two of you as soon he's back in the office. I'm virtually on my own, apart from Florence, who sits at the switchboard outside. Andy cannot commit to working a big case until he can leave his wife with the little one. He started training Florence to do some simple research before little Austin was born…'

Andy's wife had given birth to their first child not too long ago and Lerato was carrying most of the workload right now. 'Ah well, Andy has promised to take over after the big murder case.'

'That sounds like a good reason, I guess. But I still can't see how I can help you.'

'Come on now. How often must I say it? I need your talent… we need your talent.'

'So Andy knows all about me and how we solved the Misra case?'

'Of course, he does. And he's on board with it.'

'He is?' Charlie was surprised. Using a hunch in investigations was still frowned upon. In the States, where Charlie had grown up and also in South Africa. Things were evolving very slowly. One day perhaps…

'Well yes, I already told you: it was Andy's idea to involve you this time. So what's the verdict?' Lerato pushed on.

Charlie thought for a moment. 'Jono is in Durban at a friend's wedding until Monday. So I can't go anywhere because of the house and the dogs…' It sounded like a lame excuse and Lerato immediately came up with a solution.

'I'll come to you and we can talk about the case. I've got a meeting at the university with this Prof. Deon de Vries and Dr. Thokozo Sibanda." Lerato read from her notes. "That's the head of the department and his official assistant. Sibanda was part of the research team in the Kruger. It would be great if you could come with me. We can go to the bush when your brother is back from Durban.'

Clearly, Lerato didn't take 'no' for an answer and Charlie was about to cave in when her two pooches, Billie and Popcorn jumped up and raced out of the kitchen and down the driveway to bark at someone walking past. Charlie peeked through the window.

As every morning, the old lady from across the road was on her way to the park with two rather big dogs off the leash. As soon as the dog choir started, Charlie called her two rascals inside but as usual, they didn't listen. She whistled, but the barking continued.

'What's going on there?' Lerato asked.

'Sorry, it's that horrible old woman with her dogs again.' Charlie Proudfoot cried into the phone. 'Must get my doggies back inside, before they get attacked or the hag starts hitting them. Phone you back just now.'

She dropped the phone on the table and ran out into the driveway.

"Billie, Popcorn," she called and followed up with a piercing whistle. She had to call a few times before her fur-babies decided to listen. Ever since the new neighbours across the street had moved in, it had become an almost daily ritual in the Proudfoot household. The two big dogs had bitten Billie a couple of times through the gate and the old woman was not in control of them.

Jono had spoken to her granddaughter, who owned the property about the problem. But despite assurances that the dogs would be taken on a leash, it hadn't happened. Finally, Charlie's two pooches came running and she closed the kitchen gate.

"Good boy, good girl," she praised them and took a small bag off the shelf behind the kitchen door. "Who wants a treat?"

In a split second, both dogs sat down in front of

her. "I see. So, are you going to listen better the next time I call you?"

Billie held her head at an angle and looked up at Charlie with large puppy eyes as if to say: "What are you waiting for, lady? Can we have our snacks now please?"

Charlie sighed. "I guess Jono would be better at this. You listen when he calls."

She gave them their treats, opened the kitchen gate and threw a toy up the driveway after making sure that the neighbour-lady had disappeared around the corner. She never seemed to give the racket she caused with the dogs in the neighbourhood another thought. Wonder if the hag is senile, Charlie thought unkindly as she heard other dogs barking. Then she remembered with a start that she was supposed to phone Lerato back.

Should she take on another murder case? She pondered the question while dialling her friend's number. Wild dog conservation and a scientist had been killed in the Kruger Park. Hmm, a worthwhile effort, perhaps. Here she lived in a city, where crime existed in abundance, yet Lerato's cases seemed to be taking her everywhere but Johannesburg.

'Hey Lerato, it's me. Things are back to normal here.'

'Good to hear it. Is that horrible woman still yanking your chain?'

'Unfortunately.'

'By the way, you do know that you can take your cell phone with you if you walk out of the room?" Lerato complained.

'Oops sorry - haven't had a cell phone for so long that I clean forgot.'

'Well next time don't just drop the call,' Lerato mumbled.

'I'll try to remember it.'

'Come, work with me on this case, doll. You need something to do and keep your mind well-oiled,' Lerato tried to convince her. '…and I could really use your help. What better way to combine what we both need?' She tried to sound convincing.

'Alright, you win' Charlie sighed. 'But it better be simple and easy and not dangerous, please. I don't appreciate attempts on my life.' Charlie sat down on the carpet and clamped the cell phone under her chin so that she could drink from her teacup. Rooibos tea, her favourite.

'Sure love, I'll keep you safe. Remember, I have a

black belt and carry a gun."

'I've heard that one before. The criminals on the coast didn't seem to care much about your black belt and your gun.'

Lerato ignored Charlie's grumbling remark. 'Super duper. I'll pop around just now so we can make a plan. See you in about – let's say half an hour...' Charlie put the cup back onto the coffee table.

'When did you say you have that meeting at the university tomorrow?'

But Lerato had already hung up. "Great, Charlie. So much for standing your ground," she said to herself.

Kruger Park or not, murder cases gave her goosebumps. She didn't like dead bodies or anything to do with death - especially not after what happened to her husband Colin. The horrific accident that had killed him and landed her up in hospital for weeks... The insulin resistance she'd suffered as a result of the shock was still all too real. "That reminds me... I need to eat a snack."

Okay, so she'd help Lerato with another murder case. Not as safe as a job in the laboratory, but a job nonetheless. Plus, how could she say no to one of her oldest friends? And Lerato had a point. It felt good to put murderers behind bars.

They had prevented a ruthless killer from carrying out his gruesome plan before, just that this time, the murder had already been committed and she hadn't dreamt about the bush or African wild dogs or murder.

She would help Lerato with her murder case, but without her dreams, where should she even begin to find the killer of a famous zoologist?

Chapter TWO

"Could you repeat this slowly for us, please?" Charlie Proudfoot asked. She tried not to look at the crime scene photographs on the table.

The victim had been bludgeoned to death, lying head-down on the slope with his sunhat crumpled and smudged nearby. A gaping wound at the back of the man's head, encrusted with caked blood and dirt and bloodstains on the ground. Gruesome. The scene was etched on her mind and she didn't have to see it again.

Lerato and Charlie were sitting at a massive wooden table in a meeting room at the university. The head of the faculty had hired the Maitirelo Private Investigation Agency and his expectations were high. Adjacent to the meeting room was an office with a friendly secretary behind the reception desk and droopy pot plants in front of the window.

The brass sign on the heavy wooden door read:

Zoological Sciences

Dean of the Faculty

Professor Deon de Vries

Everything felt a little sticky in this room as if the furniture and the green linoleum floor hadn't been cleaned for a while. Even the crime scene photographs, the police had made available, were sticking to the table surface.

"What would you like me to repeat, Miss Proudfoot?" Professor de Vries asked with a sigh.

Dr. Thokozo Sibanda had left them about five minutes ago to give a lecture. He had answered their questions, clearing his throat often. Lerato had taken his statement, with Charlie studying his face and movements the whole time. This had made him visibly nervous. But was this nervousness an indication of guilt?

"The part where you told us about why wild dogs change dens," Charlie said and stifled a yawn. "I understand that a litter is a rare event and the dogs were looking for a new home. Isn't that the reason why our murder victim ventured out so late in the day? To monitor their movements?"

"Yes, that's why he was out there," the professor answered.

"I'm just trying to get a clearer picture of why he

was out there that day."

The two scientists had already given them a lecture about the WDOG research project. Professor Morton was no rookie. He'd been leading research teams to the Kalahari Desert and the Kruger Park on a shoestring budget for five years. They were observing the African wild dog populations to figure out how to best help them survive. The project was funded locally, but they tried to step up the funding. Deon de Vries cleared his throat and was set to comply with Charlie's request, but Lerato intervened.

"As interesting as it is, I believe we should rather focus on the witnesses. We have Dr. Sibanda's version of events, but we must also speak to the other members of the expedition."

She leaned forward on her elbows. The Dean sat between her and Charlie at the head of the table. A large whiteboard behind him was scribbled with sketches of the locations in the Kruger national Park, courtesy of Dr. Sibanda.

"Yes, yes of course." Professor de Vries was a middle-aged man with a receding hairline and a slight paunch. He had taken off his stiff grey jacket and rolled up his shirt sleeves. The pictures of the research team members were scattered next to the crime scene photos.

"The members of the expedition team will oblige, I'm sure. Ask Prudence for their contact details," he said. "The police have already taken their statements, but it's best if you ask them your own questions."

"Sure, we'll do that." Lerato picked up the copy of the initial police report. It was only 3 pages long.

"This was not the first time Prof. Morton has led a research team into the bush," de Vries said. "There have already been two other research trips to the area this year, and we regularly receive reports on the packs in the Kruger from rangers and volunteers. He knew what he was doing."

Charlie was getting the impression that they were missing an important detail. "Why do you think he didn't take somebody with him that afternoon?" She asked. "Isn't there some sort of protocol to avoid such… incidents?"

"Well, no, not really. Perhaps the other team members will be able to enlighten you on that point. If you don't mind, I can give you only a few more minutes. Unfortunately, I have another meeting scheduled with the faculty board. Is there anything else in particular that you need?"

"I just have one more question," Charlie said out of the blue. "Professor de Vries, why did you involve a private detective agency? Wouldn't it be better to deal with the homicide detectives directly?"

Something about the case began to irk her terribly, but she couldn't quite put her finger on it. Lerato kicked her casually under the table and smiled at the professor.

Charlie pulled her legs back and looked at him innocently.

"Isn't it obvious?" The Dean answered. "There is much at stake here. We need quick results and our police force is anything but quick. Call it impatience, but our next fundraising event is already scheduled. We must raise funds so we can continue with our work. A murder case does not look very good on our record and might put off a number of philanthropists with deep pockets. You are American, aren't you?"

"Well I grew up in New York…" Charlie explained. She still sounded South African, but an American accent managed to creep in now and again.

"Then you'll understand that the country's reputation

is not the best when it comes to crime."

"Well yes, I do. However,…" Charlie began.

"Thank you for being so frank with us, professor," Lerato cut in. "We promise we'll do our best."

"Anything else?" Deon de Vries stood up.

"Should we know about any behind-the-scenes facts? The more we know upfront, the quicker we can solve this murder."

"I'm not sure I understand what you're getting at. Behind the scenes?" He asked, but the Dean's face told a different story.

"We are looking for motive. Were there any animosities between colleagues or the team members in particular? Jealousy, arguments or threats… that sort of thing."

Professor de Vries played with his pen and pondered the question for a moment.

"Well, Prof. Morton's ex-wife, Jeanne Ash-Morton, who is a botanist and tenured professor at our university, comes to mind." Obviously not something he wanted to talk about. "I thought the two of them had worked things out after the divorce."

"When did they get divorced?"

"I think it's five or six years now. The divorce was amicable and they even worked on a project together…" He picked up his silver pen.

"Yes?"

"It came to my attention that there were a few hefty arguments, but I wouldn't know what they were about. Perhaps you should ask Dr. Sibanda. They knew each other… socially, you know."

"Do you know your staff socially, professor?" Lerato asked.

"Good Lord, no," he answered quickly and seemed almost offended. "I have enough on my plate trying to keep things going in this faculty. I don't have time to socialise with colleagues. My cats are all the social interaction I need after a long day at work. Now if you will excuse me, I must get to my next meeting. It's rather important."

"Thank you for your time, professor. We may have to call on you again, soon."

"Yes, yes of course. Speak to Prudence and make an appointment… I'll give you my cell phone number as well. Sorry, I'm out of business cards."

He scribbled a phone number on a piece of paper and

handed it to Lerato.

"If you can think of anything else, anything that might be relevant to the case, please contact us."

Lerato pulled out one of her business cards and handed it to Professor de Vries. He put it in his shirt pocket and nearly left his jacket behind when he walked to the door.

"Of course, I will," he said. "And please report to me directly, should you make any progress in the case. I'd much appreciate it if you could keep certain details between us." He saw his jacket on the chair and sprinted back.

"What about the police, sir?" Lerato objected. "We were assigned to an inspector Marius Vorster. His unit will have to know when we find important evidence."

"Ah yes well, of course, you must cooperate with the police but…we all know what the police are like. Please inform me first if there is any development in the case. Thank you. I must go now. Prudence will set something up if you wish. Good day to you."

He retrieved his jacket and was out of the door.

"Something is off here," Charlie said once the door closed. "I'm pretty sure he knows what's going on behind the scenes. He doesn't want to get involved because of his reputation with management."

"And his cats…" Lerato chuckled. "What a stiff."

"Lol… how on earth does he expect us to find the killer quickly if he's not open with us? We're wasting time looking in all the wrong places."

"So, he's hired us to make him look good in the eyes of his donors. We'll do what we have to do and get more information, you'll see. And you are our secret weapon."

"I'm glad to be of service." Charlie grinned. "But right now, I just feel confused."

"We just have to ease into the case. What do you think of Dr. Sibanda?" Lerato asked. "Anything that jumps out at you?"

"Dr. Sibanda is telling the truth, I'm pretty sure of it."

"Okay good. That's something. We don't have a motive yet and who but the team at the camp had an opportunity to murder our victim? They were in the bush with nobody around that we know of."

"Except for rangers, locals and tourists," Charlie said.

"True, but it's not exactly in the middle of Joburg.

And where is the motive?" Lerato sighed.

"Let's feel out the witnesses then things will become clearer."

"True. There are so many questions. How could the killer have known where to find the victim - and that he was alone? Why did he have a sprained ankle and dried blood on his elbows and his shin? Did somebody chase him? Are there defensive wounds?" She pushed the photographs on the table around.

"And a 10-year-old could have put that police report together," she grumbled.

"Let's tackle one question at the time," Charlie said. "We won't get those answers from our witnesses if they weren't there when it happened."

"The pictures don't tell me anything. Can't you touch them and get a vision or something like that?"

"Lerato… if I knew how to do that, I would've done it already. Let's start with some facts and get into things like that later."

"We keep coming back to the witnesses," Lerato decided. "Let's ask Prudence for their details. Maybe she can make some calls and off we go."

The secretary proved to be helpful. She phoned Irina

Lotcombe, the grad student, who'd been with Dr. Sibanda when they found the murder victim.

"She'll be here just now. Let me try the others on your list."

Before she could do so, Irina arrived. She had been receiving counselling and snivelled as she walked into the meeting room. A pretty dark-haired woman of slight build and sagging shoulders.

"That night, I tried to radio Prof," she explained. "For half an hour or so before we decided to search for him. It was getting dark and hardly any moonlight. We knew more or less where to look for him. Thokozo and I took the bakkie and went down the dirt road. We saw his jeep by the edge of the slope."

"Then what happened?" Lerato asked.

"We parked next to the jeep, but Prof was nowhere in sight. We looked around and then… I saw him. I saw his feet first. He was lying head down on the slope. He had blood on the back of his head and there was more on the ground. It was awful."

"Yes?"

Irina Lotcombe cried a little and dried her tears with a paper tissue before she continued. "I think I screamed.

Thokozo came running and shone his torchlight where I pointed. Then he also saw him. It was clear that we couldn't help him. His head was bashed in and one of Prof's boots was tied to his belt." She sniffled.

"At first, we didn't know what to do. Thokozo told me to contact the rangers and the camp. He went to search the area with his torch. The equipment was down by the trees." The tears rolled again.

Lerato handed her a dry tissue that soon landed on top of a small heap of wet ones. "Miss Lotcombe, is there anything you can tell us about the atmosphere at the camp? Any arguments?"

"You think it was one of us?" Irina flared up.

"It's my job to ask these questions, Ms Lotcombe."

"No, nothing at the camp. Prof was such a nice man…" she cried and Lerato handed her a new tissue. "He had some kind of problem with his ex-wife before we left. At least that's what I heard through the grapevine. I was busy during the trip. We all were. In the beginning, we had a little argument because I forgot to bring my own torchlight. Nothing serious, I would have remembered that."

"Do you know what Prof. Morton and his ex-wife

were fighting about?"

"I think it was about some kind of project."

"But Mrs. Ash-Morton is a botanist, isn't she?"

"Yes, she is." Irina dabbed her eyes with a new tissue. "I'm in a different faculty, so we don't interact much. But yes, as far as I know, the project had something to do with plants." She added the soggy tissue to the heap on the table.

"I see." Lerato gave the student her number. "If there is anything else you can remember, please let us know." The grad student left the room, still sniffling.

"That confirms Dr. Sibanda's account of events," Charlie said.

"We should speak to him again. Maybe he's done with his lecture by now. Let me ask the secretary." Within five minutes, the scientist was back in the meeting room. "Prudence says you have more questions?"

"We just spoke to Irina Lotcombe and perhaps you could fill in some gaps for us."

"Certainly. What would you like to know?"

"This project the Mortons were working on… can you tell us more about it?"

"You mean because they were arguing before we left

for the Kruger?"

"Yes."

"It was the first time I'd heard them argue in Prof's office. My office is just down the passage, so I couldn't help overhearing… I assume it was about the patent."

"The patent?" Lerato asked him.

"For the project. When I asked Gerald why they were arguing he clammed up."

"Any idea what the patent could have been for?"

"Some plant formula. As I said, Gerald didn't want to talk about it. Why don't you ask Jeanne, herself?"

"The ex-wife… Jeanne Ash-Morton?" Lerato asked.

He looked at his watch. "She's probably in her office right now. It's in the same building. Just the floor above us. Her office is at the end of the passage…" He gestured with his hands. Lerato repeated the routine with her phone number and Dr. Sibanda promised to give her a call if he could think of anything else.

"I really need to get more business cards," Lerato said after he'd left the room.

Charlie sighed deeply. "What are they hiding?"

"The Dean and Dr. Sibanda?" Lerato probed. "Or the student? What did I bring you for? Didn't you pick anything up?”

“No, I just have a strange feeling about everything. Maybe it has to sit with me for a while.” She swept her hair back.

“Well, don’t take too long. You heard the Dean: they have this fundraiser coming up and he needs results soon.”

“Sure, I’ll just press a button and my intuitiveness-computer will spit out the right answer.” Charlie rolled her eyes.

“You’re cooked, doll!” Lerato chuckled.

“Let me sleep on it then. Do you want to pay the other Professor Morton a visit?”

“Professor Ash-Morton, doll. Probably not a bad idea, what do you think?” Lerato started packing up the photographs and the police report.

“Why not? Let’s find her office. Then we are done here and can question the other witnesses. Did Prudence give you their contact details?” Charlie asked.

“Yes, let’s see…” Lerato studied her notes. “I believe the volunteer, Pericles Duncey, lives not far from here, in Westcliff. Posh area. Let’s go and see him first. Dr. Nivedna Naidoo’s clinic‘s in Blairgowrie.

We'll go there afterwards. My goodness, is that the time already?" Lerato checked her cell phone and quickly stuffed the last of the crime scene photos into her bag.

"Yup, 11:30," Charlie said. "Why? Seems like the perfect time to me."

"It's time for a snack, my girl. We want to reverse your diabetes, remember? You look a little hungry to me. Have some peanuts. Here."

"Okay, Mom. I'll have some peanuts."

Lerato took out a packet she had brought for her friend and shook some peanuts into Charlie's hand. "And here is an apple. What would you do without me, Ms. Proudfoot?"

"I can't imagine." Charlie grinned and began to eat the nuts when the door to the meeting room opened.

"Are you the private detectives?" A tall, blond woman in a hound's tooth suit asked and walked in without further ado. "Prudence told me you're here."

"Yes, but we were about to leave," Lerato answered. "I'm Lerato Gwala, Private Investigator. This is my associate Charlotte Proudfoot. And you are…?"

"My name is Jeanne Ash-Morton. Professor Jeanne Ash-Morton and I'd like a word with you."

Chapter THREE

"Mrs. Ash-Morton… now that's a surprise. We were on our way to you…." Lerato stuttered before checking herself. "But since you are here already, please have a seat." Charlie and Lerato sat down again and turned their chairs so that they faced the botany expert. The elegant blonde woman took a seat at the other end of the table. It was obvious that her hair had been coiffed at a very expensive salon.

"We are sorry for your loss," Charlie said. "I also recently lost my husband and I know how difficult…"

"He was my ex-husband, so no need to be overly sentimental," the woman interrupted and Charlie recoiled. "Excuse me for coming here on the spur of the moment. You must be busy, but I wanted to give you my side of the story before you got the wrong impression."

"I see, and what impression would that be?" Lerato asked her in the same matter-of-fact tone.

Charlie didn't know what to do with the peanuts in

her fist, so she bent down as if she was looking for something under the table. She put the nuts in her mouth, sat up and chewed them as discreetly as possible while scribbling down notes.

"That I might have something to do with my ex-husband's death," the woman clarified. Her harsh expression relaxed a little.

Lerato and Charlie looked at each other. There was not a tear in Mrs. Morton's eye. Charlie's alarm bells had gone off the moment she began speaking. *What have you got to hide*, she thought and dropped the apple she had intended to eat into her Mary Poppins bag.

"Let's not beat around the bush, then. Do you have anything at all to do with your husband's death, Mrs. Ash-Morton?" Lerato asked bluntly. Charlie studied the interaction, still chewing the peanuts.

"Don't be ridiculous!" Jeanne Ash-Morton blurted out. She emphasized the word ridiculous and held herself stiffly upright. It was clear that this woman didn't take anything lying down.

"Why would that be ridiculous?" Lerato kept the pressure on. "We've been told that the two of you had a few heated arguments of late. Specifically, before the research team left for the Kruger Park."

"Yes well… that… well, it was nothing serious." The woman seemed surprised by the question. "First of all," she continued in a firm tone, "I was nowhere near the Kruger Park when this… this death happened and secondly, we were just arguing over a work project. We decided to develop a product together and Gerald wanted a greater say than was appropriate, just decided to do his own thing. It wasn't fair."

"Can you tell us what this project is all about? What kind of a product you developed together?"

"I can't give you the exact details for obvious reasons, but it involves a revolutionary, new type of medicine that is derived from a plant only found in Southern Africa and Madagascar. This new medicine has the potential to make us very rich."

"And now you're the only beneficiary of those potential proceeds?" Lerato probed.

"Well no… no, I'm not. The patent is still pending and the development and testing don't come cheap, so there are other investors. Pericles Duncey, for example. He is one of the wild dog conservation's staunchest supporters and often volunteers to go on expeditions. He's inherited a great deal of money from his uncle in the US, I think, and wants to put it to good use. Then Herbert Mosely, a philanthropist and investor from New York with a special interest in Africa. He is also a relative of the US president and very influential. There are others, most of them Gerald's contacts, so why would I want to harm Gerald?"

"People do the strangest things," Charlie said. She had eaten her peanuts and retrieved the apple from her bag. It sat in front of her on the exam pad.

"Yes maybe… but not me. I know how this must look to you, but I can assure you that I'm not gaining anything from Gerald's death. Our investors are coming to the fundraiser and we would have worked things out eventually."

"So the event at the end of the month is equally important to you?" Charlie said and scribbled on the pad.

"Well yes. Two birds with one stone, in a manner of speaking."

"Right. We would need a list of current and potential investors, then. Can you tell us anything about your ex-husband that might give his killer a motive?" Lerato asked.

"Very well – and no, there is nothing I can think of. He was a hardworking academic who loved the outdoors and wanted to make this planet a better place. I wish I could help you find the killer. I really do."

"Apart from the fact that he wanted a bigger piece of the pie," Lerato drilled down.

"I wouldn't put it that way. You make it sound so tacky." There was this harsh tone again. For a moment, Charlie thought the woman would show some degree of grief.

"Hmm yes. If you don't mind my asking, what led to your divorce four years ago or was it five years?" Lerato peppered the next question at the professor.

"Six years – and isn't that a bit of a personal question? I mean I'm not even a suspect in this case, so why would you want to know why Gerald and I called it quits?"

"It's quite relevant under the circumstances, don't you think? In a murder investigation everything, even the smallest detail can be relevant, Mrs. Morton."

"It's Ash-Morton…"

"Sorry. Ms Ash-Morton."

"Very well. I had an affair with one of Gerald's

friends and he found out. He was always so wrapped up in his work. There wasn't much time for a wife, never mind a family. I found out later that endometriosis was an obstacle to motherhood, but of course, in his eyes, I didn't want children because of my own career."

"Did you ever regret having divorced your husband?"

"There are always regrets. He couldn't get over my cheating and it was too much of an effort to work on our relationship after such a deal-breaker. He just couldn't handle the realities of a human relationship and change doesn't exist in his world. That's why I wanted out in the end. Despite all of this, I did love him at some level…"

That's hard to believe, Charlie thought fleetingly and eyed her apple. She was hungry and this meeting went on and on.

"I see. What's the name of the man you cheated with?"

"I don't see that it has anything to do with Gerald's murder."

"Please answer the question," Lerato insisted.

Jeanne Ash-Morton took a deep breath. It was clear that she had come to make a point and didn't like being questioned very much. This question was certainly ruffling her feathers. "Okay then… it was Dr. Sibanda. And it was only a very brief fling, but Gerald took the betrayal so much to heart," she said and rolled her eyes. "I don't know why I ever told him."

"Dr. Thokozo Sibanda?" Lerato sounded surprised. "Isn't he married?"

"Yes, now he is. It was a long time ago. So you see, it doesn't matter anymore."

Lerato recovered quickly. "Can you tell us about other relationships both of you had after the divorce? Anything that stands out? Jealousy perhaps?"

"Jealousy? Sure. The great Professor Gerald Morton fighting for his wife. That's a joke. We were better off as friends and colleagues, believe me."

"And… was there anybody else in the picture in those six years?"

"My husband had a few dalliances with women after the divorce. Shelley, Amanda, Faith… to name a few. Those are names I can remember. They never lasted. On my side, I had a long-distance relationship with an Irish researcher I'd met at a conference in France. But that's been over for a year. Nothing serious since then."

She sighed in frustration.

"Could you please give us the names and contact details of those persons you do remember?"

"You have to ask Dr. Sibanda. That's his department. He was friends with my husband and can give you a great deal more information on this than I could."

"We spoke to him just now, but he didn't mention anything about girlfriends."

"He also didn't mention our affair, did he?"

"No, he didn't. Very well, then just the names of your own… contacts, please." Lerato gave the professor a pen. The woman wrote down a couple of names and details and handed the paper back to Lerato. "That's all for now. Thank you for coming by, Professor Ash-Morton."

Lerato scribbled her phone number down and the woman studied the writing for a moment before putting the scrap of paper in her pocket. "I'll give you a call, should I remember anything important," she said. "Goodbye, ladies."

Her movements were very controlled as she walked out of the meeting room. Charlie's last impression of the academic was the back of the hound's tooth suit, shapely legs and high-heeled shoes.

"Now that was unexpected," Lerato said and stood up. "But just as well. Those relationships sound complicated. Dr. Sibanda and her... that's hard to believe. He seems quite warm and she has not an emotional bone in her body."

"She's definitely not in love with her ex-husband." Charlie took the apple and bit into the tart fruit. "I don't trust her."

"That makes two of us."

"Hmm, why would she seek us out just to say that she had nothing to do with the murder? She provided an alibi into the deal before we had a chance to ask," Charlie said. "And I'm sure that there are more lovers than she lets on."

Lerato was ready to go. "At least it saves us time. We can keep an eye on her and she goes onto the suspect list. Actually, we can tell our friends in the police to keep an eye on her. We have more suspects to interview. Now eat your apple. If we make it to Pericles Duncey before lunchtime, we can get a proper bite to eat after our visit to Dr. Naidoo."

"Duncey inherited money from his uncle...

interesting that a volunteer is one of the main investors in their project," Charlie said as they walked out of the room.

"Keeping it in the family. I'll ask Florence to do some research on Duncey and Herbert Mosely, the philanthropist guy from New York. Let's see what she turns up."

*

Google Maps took them to a mansion in the leafy suburb of Westcliff. They drove past stately homes, seemingly untouched by time.

"My goodness, compared to this, we have virtually no security at home," Charlie said a wide-eyed. "27, 29, 31. There it is… number 31 - the white wall and green gate."

The house was surrounded by a flower-filled garden that appeared to burst at the seams. Red bougainvillaea grew into the trees and dripped over the high wall. Security in this upmarket area was of a high standard with lots of cameras atop spiked walls and electric fencing.

Pericles Duncey's home was no different and two security cameras picked up their arrival at the gate.

"You know that this doesn't deter criminals

much." Lerato snorted and drove up to the green gate. "The more security, the more of a dare for them to get in. Behind high walls is the promise of valuable loot."

She pressed the intercom button and three melodious ringtones reverberated off-pitch. The intercom crackled.

"Hello," a woman answered in a stern voice.

"Ms. Gwala and Ms. Proudfoot from Maitirelo. We are here to see Mr. Pericles Duncey, please."

A bird sang a rather insistent melody in a tree covered in purple flowers.

"Do you have an appointment with Mr. Duncey?" The voice asked in a haughty tone. Lerato rolled her eyes and answered politely.

"No we don't, but Professor de Vries sent us…"

There was an immediate click and the gate hummed open.

"Hmm, open sesame," Charlie Proudfoot chuckled.

"Let's hope this is worth our time and Mr. Duncey can give us some answers."

That, Mr. Duncey could do. He was an old-school English gentleman in his mid-forties, wearing slacks and an expensive tennis-shirt. His face was flushed from the midday heat and topped by floppy blond hair. Mr. Duncey appeared slightly twitchy but undoubtedly in a good mood as he met them on the gravelled driveway.

"Welcome, ladies. What a cute little car. Real private detectives if I'm not mistaken! Word travels fast, but who knew detectives could be so good-looking," he warbled and led them along a flower-border into the house.

"I will answer your burning questions. Anything you need to know that I haven't told the country police already. Anything to find who did this to our Prof - God rest his soul." There was a hint of sarcasm in his voice that was puzzling, but they decided to ignore it for now.

"Good day, Mr. Duncey, thank you for seeing us," Lerato greeted him and Charlie just nodded. "We do appreciate your time."

They entered the salon followed closely by the rather strict-looking housekeeper. Her hair was up in a tight bun at the nape of her neck and she wore a plain grey dress. Pericles Duncey waved her out of the room almost immediately.

"Off you go my precious worker bee, attend to your household duties." He winked at his visitors in a conspiratorial way that made them cringe with embarrassment. "Bring us some tea … or would the ladies prefer coffee?"

"Tea will be fine," Lerato answered slowly.

For the life of her, she could not imagine this somewhat effeminate man doing volunteer work with wild dogs, roughing it in the bush replete with dirt and bugs. She gave Charlie a vexed look while they stood in the middle of the room. Their suspect gestured at two flowery chairs opposite the sofa covered in a similar fabric.

"Please have a seat."

The interior was old-fashioned with pastoral scenes in golden frames decorating the pastel green walls. He lived with his mother and it was likely that the elusive old woman had chosen the decorations.

Duncey plopped himself onto the sofa and put his arm leisurely on the backrest. Then he looked out into his garden. "Look at these wonderful flowers… to think that winter is coming so soon makes me a little sad."

He turned abruptly to face his visitors.

The impulsive movement loosened a long strand of blond hair. He pushed his hair back into shape and stared out of the window again.

"Fortunately, our winters are mild and short," Charlie said politely.

"Could we ask you a few questions, please?" Lerato came to the point. "Can you tell us what happened during your last trip to the Kruger Park? We understand you were a volunteer on the research team."

"Certainly," he said.

"Specifically what happened on the last day," Lerato clarified in a professional tone. "Anything that has to do with…"

"You mean the murder of poor Prof Morton?" Mr. Duncey interrupted her. "So sad. Yes of course, ladies. Ask away. Anything I can do to help."

They looked at each other. Had he not heard Lerato's question? He put his feet on a striped ottoman that stood between him and his visitors. A young shepherd girl stared at them with empty eyes from the painting behind him.

"Now where is Janet with that tea I asked for?" He turned towards the door and frowned.

"Yes, the murder of Professor Morton," Lerato reigned his attention back in. "Please tell us what happened from your point of view." Pericles Duncey seemed easily distracted. She held her pen up. "Ready when you are."

"Certainly," the man on the sofa repeated with knitted eyebrows. He tried to remember then spoke rapidly without taking a breath. His account did not vary much from the other statements so far. He let out a sigh of relief and said something that made them sit up.

"If you ask me, there is something between Doc Sibanda and this student, Irina."

"Oh? Why would you say that?" Charlie asked.

The housekeeper brought in the tea and waited for him to take his feet off the ottoman before putting the silver tray down.

"Janet, be so kind and take a cup of Oolong with some biscotti up to mother's room, will you?"

"Yes, Mr. Duncey." The housekeeper poured the amber liquid into – wonder oh wonder - floral cups.

Duncey waited for the unsmiling woman to leave the room before he answered Charlie's question. "They went to the crime scene together, didn't they?"

He chuckled as if he was telling them a juicy secret.

"Hello!" He smirked and produced juice from a slice of lemon with one of those little presses they have in high-end coffee shops. "If that doesn't tell you something…"

"So, that's why you think there might be something going on between the two of them?" Charlie frowned. "Because they went to look for Professor Morton that night?"

"No, that's not everything, of course." Mr. Duncey guffawed. He picked up his cup and slurped the lemony tea. "Help yourselves to milk and sugar if you prefer that."

"I'm sorry but I'm confused, sir. What other reason lets you assume such a thing?"

"Because they seem rather friendly with each other and ALWAYS work together." He slurped more of his tea, still looking at them.

"But Miss Lotcombe also works with the vet, Dr. Naidoo, and everybody else on the team, doesn't she?" Lerato stopped taking notes. "Nobody else mentioned this and I don't see what it could possibly have to do with the murder."

"Hmm, probably nothing," He said lightly.

A long-haired white cat jumped onto the window sill outside and sneaked into the room through an open window.

"Ah there you are, Bambi," he greeted his pet and the ghost-like animal weaved through his legs, which made him giggle. Bambi hissed at the visitors before disappearing through an open French door into the next room.

"Isn't she just adorable?" He set down his teacup and smiled.

"Yes. Back to my question, sir. Has this… observation of yours anything to do with a possible motive for the murder? Jealousy, perhaps?"

"Motive? Let me think… Prof Morton was way too busy with his work to care about the girl, but they could have cooked something up. Doc and the student."

"Sir, I don't understand. Cook what up?"

"Don't mind me. It's none of my business anyway," he said lightly, brushing his disturbing remark aside with a hand movement.

I'll say, Charlie thought. This man gave her an uncomfortable feeling. "Tell us, Mr. Duncey, how come you do volunteer work for this project? Do you enjoy camping in the bush, monitoring a pack of wild dogs?" She asked.

"Enjoy? No, of course not. I'm not exactly enjoying the outdoors, but somebody has to do it or those poor animals will disappear before soon."

"That's very noble of you," Lerato said.

"It's the privilege of a major donor to go with the team and sometimes it's the only way to get away from my mother."

"Your mother?"

He giggled and covered his mouth with his hand like a naughty little boy. Then he caught himself and continued to speak in a measured tone.

"Rhinos and elephants are too big and scary for me, so wild dogs are just the right size. As long as I don't have to touch them, I'm quite happy to be there. I'm usually the one, who holds up the antenna for Prof, while the others write things down. I even named one of the male dogs Harry."

He swung his legs up onto the ottoman next to the silver tray and folded his hands behind his head. "His fur has a ginger hue."

"Right," Charlie said. "So you are funding the wild dog conservation project?"

He made a little bow. "Yes, but not entirely. And we need more donors now if we want to make progress."

"We were told that you inherited money from your uncle. Could you tell us more about that?"

"My uncle? Yes, he was quite wealthy, the old bastard. John Brewster. Oil in Oklahoma... who knew, right?! Left half of his fortune to an animal charity in his estate and the rest to me and mother. Bless him."

"John Brewster, I see. You are also investing in a project by Prof. Morton and his ex-wife, aren't you? Something to do with desert plants and a new type of medicine..." Lerato said and studied his face.

"Yes, that's correct. Mother and I are fascinated by this project. The future of medicine if you ask me. Although I'm not formally trained in the field, I absolutely believe in research and finding new remedies for ailments. It's a worthy cause to invest in, don't you think? Who told you about our project if I may ask?"

"Prof. Ash-Morton told us. She mentioned your name as an investor together with a Mr. Mosely."

"Did she now?" He scoffed. "Mosely opted out this morning. He sold his share to my cousin, William Brewster. The lawyers are doing the transfer right now." He winked at Lerato. "We are putting old uncle John's fortune to good use. Bless him that he didn't gamble it all away while he was alive."

"Can you tell us more about this rather interesting plant project, Mr. Duncey?"

"I'm afraid, I'm not supposed to divulge any details about the project until all the 'i's are dotted and all the 't's are crossed. There is a patent pending. And I'm not an expert in any case. You do understand that, don't you?"

"Yes, Mr. Duncey, we do. We are only interested in solving the murder of Professor Morton and if there is a connection to this project, we'd like to know," Lerato said. "Could you give us the names of the investors in the project, please?"

Duncey rattled off the names. Mrs. Alice Duncey, his mother, was also on the rather short list. Lerato wrote down the names.

Charlie wondered why there was neither giggling nor weird allegations from this rich man, now that they were no longer talking about Professor Morton.

Was he putting on an act?

"Jeanne Ash-Morton runs the scientific side of things and now that her ex-husband is dead, she has sole control of the project in that respect. She loves to show us her graphs and pictures, not that I understand much. Jeanne keeps all the documents under lock and key in her desk. You should ask her about that."

"We will, sir, once we've spoken to all the suspects…"

"You're not saying that I'm a suspect, are you?"

"It's just a professional term. It doesn't mean that we believe you did it. Perhaps I should say that we need to speak to everybody who was on the expedition in the Kruger Park."

"You do that, my dear lady-detectives. Now, where is this useless housekeeper of mine?" He looked around. "In the kitchen I presume, putting together another one of her wonderful dinners." Duncey stood up. "Janet, come and take the tray away, please!"

Lerato followed suit, and Charlie looked a little confused.

"I think it's time for us to go," Lerato said. "Thank you so much, Mr. Duncey. You were a great help. We don't want to take up any more of your precious time."

"It was my pleasure. Do come again, soon. Mark me - we'll discuss a more pleasurable topic over tea on another occasion."

"For sure, we will," Charlie said amiably and pulled her hand back when he tried to smack a kiss on it. He called his housekeeper to see them out. Janet guided the two sleuths out sombrely and opened the gate for them with the click of a button.

Pericles Duncey sat down on the floral sofa and dialled a number on his cell phone.

"Hi Tom, it's me. Yes, they are leaving. Of course, they were digging," he said and stroked his cat's feathery white fur. "But don't worry, I handled it."

He ended the call, while Bambi rolled on her back, clawing his hand, purring.

*

"Why did you want to leave so abruptly?" Charlie whispered.

Lerato pressed the car remote. "Because we were wasting our time. He knows far more than he's admitting, but he won't come out with it. He was trying to send us on a wild goose chase, so why stay any longer than necessary? Had me thinking he wasn't quite right upstairs for a while."

Charlie opened the passenger door. "He acted the fool the entire time. The student and doctor Sibanda having an affair… my foot!"

"We could have tickled the information out of him."

"You mean like Chinese torture?" Charlie giggled.

"No, but he's not the first witness I've interrogated."

"So why didn't you?"

"Maybe some other time. Right now, we have another suspect to see."

"This guy likes playing the popinjay. Pfff and Dr. Sibanda would never cheat on his wife with a student."

"He wouldn't?" Lerato started the motor and turned the car around. "How do you know that? He had an affair with Prof. Morton's ex-wife."

"Yes, before he got married. I thought you brought me along for my intuitiveness. Trust me on this. And Duncey knows damn well what this project is all about. I have a feeling there is some kind of a link to our murder."

Then we must get our hands on those documents in

Mrs. Ash-Morton's desk."

"And how do you propose we do that?" Charlie asked. The iron gate hummed closed behind them.

"We'll get ourselves onto the guestlist for the fundraiser. You'll dazzle them with your superior knowledge of biology, while I disappear and gain access to that infamous desk Mr. Duncey mentioned. He thinks he got it all sorted but we'll outsmart him, you'll see. Your department is intuition, mine is sleuthing."

"Glad we got that straight."

"Alright… What does Google Maps say? Where are we going?" Lerato asked.

"Oh yes, hang on." Charlie typed in the address. "Turn left, and then straight until we get to Wicklow Road."

They drove north. "134 Morkel Crescent. Not far from the Plaza. Prudence said earlier that Dr. Nivedna Naidoo is in her surgery. I hope she didn't leave for lunch. Turn left here." Lerato turned left.

"Pericles Duncey is such an oddball," she said to Charlie. "He was born 200 years too late. I still can't visualise him with men like Prof. Morton and Dr. Sibanda out in the bush. Playing tennis at his country club? Sure, anytime, but the bush is not his first choice."

"We'll find out soon enough why he led us on. Do I turn here?"

"Go straight over the traffic lights," Charlie said. "I liked his garden, though."

Fifteen minutes later, they arrived at the animal clinic in Blairgowrie and walked into the reception. Posters of happy dogs with bowls of food and jumping for joy to fetch toys were plastered across the walls. Charlie wasn't paying attention and bumped into the cardboard cut-out of a vet holding an over-sized tube. "Ouch!"

Two dogs lay on the tiled floor and looked up tetchily, while their owners kept an eye on them with a mixture of pride and worry.

"Can we speak to Dr. Naidoo, please?" Lerato asked.

"Dr. Naidoo is seeing a patient," the receptionist said in a bored voice. She'd noticed the lack of a pet when the women walked in. "Doctor has appointments back to back until 6 o'clock."

"Until tonight? Can't we see her sooner? Ten minutes tops. It's kind of urgent."

"She won't be coming in tomorrow and will be in

surgery all morning on Thursday. Friday, perhaps?"

"That's too late. Prudence called earlier…"

"You could come back later. Half-past six?" The receptionist took out her chewing gum, rolled it in a tissue and placed it in a box under her desk. "Excuse me please." She took a piece of paper from the owner of a black cat and typed something on her computer.

The cat sat in its carry case and surveyed the waiting room with an uneasy stare. One of the dogs sat up and winced. "It's alright, Barney. It's alright," his owner fussed.

"Six hundred and thirty-five please."

The private detectives had to wait until the payment was done. They sat down on chairs facing the entrance.

"I see that one of the appointments was cancelled," the receptionist said and the two women looked up in surprise. "Let me ask Dr. Naidoo if she can see you now."

"That would be swell," Lerato said in a sarcastic tone and smiled brightly. "Please do and tell her that Professor de Vries sends us."

"Sure." The receptionist grabbed a few sheets of paper and walked graciously through the swinging doors to the consultation rooms. It took her a few minutes to return. "Dr. Naidoo can't see you today; she's busy with urgent tests." The woman said and languidly sat back down on her receptionist chair.

"Did you tell her that it's urgent?" Lerato asked.

"Yes."

"Well, when can she see us?" Lerato kept talking to the receptionist who checked her diary, and nodded towards the swinging door. Charlie understood and sneaked through the door behind her back.

She walked slowly down the passage and peered through every open door. A stocky dark-haired woman in a white coat sat at a desk in the last consultation room, writing something on a patient card.

"Are you Dr. Naidoo?" Charlie asked the woman.

"Yes, and who are you?" The vet snapped at her.

"I'm Charlie Proudfoot with the Maitirelo Agency. Professor de Vries gave us your contact details and we thought that Prudence called. We have a few questions regarding the… murder during your last trip to the Kruger Park…"

"I asked Magda to tell you that I'm busy right now! You can't just walk in here. Make an appointment," the woman grumbled and threw her pen down on the desk. Her cell phone rang and she abruptly declined the call.

"With all due respect, Dr. Naidoo, but don't you want to see this homicide solved?"

"The police in the Kruger Park have already questioned me and I told them what I know. There is no need for another interrogation by some private detectives I know nothing about."

"Prof. de Vries seems to disagree. He is the client, who hired us."

"Then go and ask him," Dr. Naidoo replied grouchily. "I don't work for him."

"We already did. But of course, he was not present, when the murder took place. That's why we were hoping you would be able to answer…"

"Well, neither was I," Dr. Naidoo interrupted Charlie. "I stayed at the camp when Irina and Thokozo went to look for Prof. So I can't tell you anything about the crime scene and what they found. They were upset. So there."

The receptionist walked in to announce the next patient. "What are you doing here?" She asked sternly. "I swear doctor, I told them…"

"It's alright Magda. Tell Mr. Helmsley to wait five

minutes.”

Magda left in a huff and Charlie grabbed the chance to ask the vet a question.

“Why are you involved in wild dog conservation if I may ask? Your surgery seems to be keeping you quite busy.”

“Mr. Duncey asked me if I wanted to get involved. I’m interested in wildlife conservation, so I said yes.”

“How do you know Mr. Duncey, doctor?”

“Bambi has been my patient for a few years now.”

“His cat?”

“Yes, his cat. Can’t say I like him very much, but there you have it.” Dr. Naidoo didn’t seem to like anybody very much.

“Can you tell me anything about the events leading up to the murder?”

“I can tell you that Prof drove to the observation spot after speaking to Thokozo about dinner. It was Thokozo’s turn to cook and he told Prof not to come back too late. Of course, we didn’t know that he would never come back at all. Very tragic. We were all in shock about what happened. There was no indication that anything was amiss when Professor

Morton left the camp. Now if you will excuse me…"

Dr. Naidoo picked up her pen and used it to point to the door.

"At what time, would you say, did they speak to each other?"

"I don't know, 4:30 maybe. It was a bit later than usual. We usually try to be back at the camp before dark, so around 6:00."

"Were there any problems between the team members and Prof?" Charlie probed further, ignoring the vet's unspoken request. "Anything you noticed that could shed some light on this case?"

"What do you mean? There were no problems. Not that I know of, anyway. It was my job to treat animals that were found injured in snares and to put collars on adult dogs and so on. So I wouldn't know about any problems. I'm not a psychologist or marriage counsellor and I had my hands full. If you will excuse me, I have important tests to conduct, until my next patient shows up." The vet waved her unwelcome visitor out with a gruff expression and began to write on her patient card again.

"Very well, Dr. Naidoo, as you wish." Charlie

Proudfoot was taken aback by the woman's rude behaviour. *Marriage counsellor...* hmm, she thought and made a mental note.

'Doctor... Mr. Helmsley is waiting with Hunny,' the receptionist's voice hissed through the intercom. 'The bleeding paw...'

'Ask Elson to bring them through to surgery no.1. I'll be there in a minute,' Dr. Naidoo answered, then turned to Charlie. "As you can see, I'm extremely busy," she hollered. "Next time, make an appointment. Good day to you, Miss, Miss..."

"Proudfoot," Charlie said. She walked down the passage and pushed the swing door to the reception wide   open.

Chapter FOUR

"Still nothing?" Lerato asked Charlie. She was referring to her friend's ability to 'feel out' a situation and to dream specifically about a case. This represented all that fuzzy stuff Lerato's trained mind could not easily tap into.

They were driving to the police headquarters in town to meet Inspector Marius Vorster of the Homicide Unit. He was the investigating officer, who had been assigned to the case by the Police Commissioner himself. It was early afternoon and they had been virtually kicked out of Dr. Nivedna Naidoo's surgery. The veterinarian had been less than forthcoming.

"If you mean my intuition, then I have nothing. I can tell that there is more to the story than our suspects are willing to tell us. I can't put my finger on it just yet… I mean you don't have to be psychic to see that she wanted to get rid of us without answering questions. That doesn't mean that I am."

"I know." A mini-van taxi cut Lerato off and then

slowed down in front of her. "Bloody idiot!"

They drove over the Mandela Bridge and the taxi soon joined the lane of cars and mini taxis heading for the taxi rank in Eloff Street. Lerato overtook the column on the right-hand side.

"Well, I hope you'll pick up on something soon. We need leads. Odd that the vet was so rude. Doesn't she have an interest in getting the killer found?"

"Duncey got her involved in the wild dog conservation, but she doesn't seem to like him very much... I wonder if that means anything."

Lerato stopped the car at a red traffic light and in the lane next to theirs, two taxis went over the crossing, hooting at cars coming towards them on the wrong side. "As long as this case doesn't turn into a hot mess, we'll know more soon."

"And if everything was so peachy, shouldn't she be collaborating with us?" Charlie closed the window on the passenger side to avoid a newspaper sales guy. "The vet said something about not being a psychologist or marriage counsellor." Lerato turned into a one-way street. What does that even mean? I have a distinct feeling that there's a cover-up. The victim's ex-wife is over-eager to prove her innocence, then Pericles Duncey tries to distract us with nonsense, and the vet doesn't want to talk to us at all."

"There you go… if you have a distinct feeling, that's good. You don't need me after all, see." Some guy held up a car license plate and gestured to Charlie that he wanted 200 Rand for it. She looked away he gestured to the car behind them.

"Nice try, Charlie." Lerato chuckled. "You are my consultant, remember? As for Professor de Vries – I wish he cared a bit more. It doesn't make sense. Why hire us and then leave us in the lurch?"

A mini taxi was cutting in in front of Lerato's car again. "Hey you damn jerk! Yesssee!" She flipped him off in good Joburg-driver fashion.

Charlie laughed. "You showed him!"

"I wish the taxi drivers in town cared. Those poor passengers are at their mercy…"

"What did you say just now?" Charlie sat up.

"I said …those passengers are at their mercy…" Lerato shrugged her shoulders.

"No, you said: I wish he cared." Charlie gesticulated. "Professor de Vries doesn't care. The question is why not? He gets us involved, and then he couldn't give a hoot whether the killer is found or not. I'll mull over that for a moment."

"You do that. It's pretty obvious that he's worried about scaring off donors. Maybe it's also professional jealousy."

"He doesn't seem to care much for our dead professor or anybody else for that matter. Cold fish if you ask me."

"Your intuition coming back?" Lerato stopped for a group of people in the street.

"Call it intuition if you like. Maybe it's just a light-bulb moment."

"At last!" Lerato cheered and high-fived her friend. "And if he doesn't care... then why not? I mean it's costing him good money. If he has doubts that we can crack the case, he's in for a surprise!"

"Exactly. But that's all I've got for you right now."

"That's better than nothing. Just look what this guy is doing: weaving in and out of traffic - as if there was enough space here!"

Lerato cursed in Xhosa at the other driver. She could get so upset about bad drivers and the centre of

Johannesburg taxi drivers were a law unto themselves.

"I swear this is the worst traffic in the world!"

"Not even Cape Town is worse?" Charlie asked innocently. They had driven around Cape Town quite a bit when working their last case and Lerato had behaved pretty much the same there.

"Okay – touché," Lerato laughed. "But at least, in Cape Town, you usually have a beautiful view." Another mini-taxi came towards them in their lane.

"Masendako!" She cursed a little less fiery and swerved just enough not to cause a collision with the negligent driver.

"We're almost there." She turned into the underground parking at the police headquarters. They went through security and Lerato parked in the space next to Inspector Vorster's spot, just because she was irritated. The parking bay was marked with the name J. Phaladi, possibly another homicide detective, but Lerato didn't care. They followed the 'Elevator' sign.

"It's over there." She pointed to a couple of silver doors that opened with a ping. "Press the button for the fifth floor, Charlie. I'm surprised that the lift works," she grumbled and leaned against the rail behind her. "It's a government building after all..."

A corpulent man, carrying a couple of blue folders, entered the lift before the door could close, and greeted them with a brief nod. "Good afternoon."

"Good afternoon," they both answered.

"Just calm down now," Charlie whispered. "You can't get upset about traffic every time we have to go and see this inspector."

The corpulent man ogled Lerato and she shot him a withering look.

"I know. So let's keep it to a minimum." Lerato turned her back to the man. Ping.

"That's the fifth floor," Charlie said. "Excuse me." They pushed past the man and stood in front of the elevators. Ping. The other elevator stopped at their floor and released two women, who were busy chatting.

"Where do we go now?" Charlie asked.

"Homicide is this way if I remember correctly," Lerato said and they trudged down the passage behind the chatting women. A reception desk came into sight.

"We are here to see Inspector Vorster, please."

"Your name is?" The receptionist asked.

"We are from the Maitirelo Agency... he is

expecting us."

The receptionist picked up the phone and announced the two women. "He'll be with you in a minute. Yes, please?" She moved onto the next person.

"Not even a chair to sit down on," Lerato grumbled. It took about a minute before a good-looking man walked through a glass door and smiled at them.

"Good day, ladies. How can I help?" Marius Vorster greeted them in the waiting area. He seemed a little puzzled to see the two women.

"Good day, inspector Vorster? I am Lerato Gwala from the Maitirelo Agency."

"Maitirelo Agency – are you here for the secretarial position?"

"…and this is my associate Charlie Proudfoot. I spoke to you earlier on the phone," Lerato continued. "We are here about the Morton murder case. And no… we are not secretaries."

"Oh dear, my apologies… you are the PI ladies! Sorry, we are having a hectic day around here. My apologies." He seemed embarrassed.

"Not to worry, inspector." Lerato decided to let the error slide, because the inspector was rather good-looking and he didn't seem to be sexist.

"This way, ladies." He opened the glass door and they followed him along a lacklustre passage to a modest office.

"Please have a seat," he said in a friendly tone. "Can I make it up to you with a cup of coffee?"

They sat down on wobbly chairs. At least there were chairs.

"You're in luck that I'm used to bad coffee," Lerato joked.

"Oh, how is that?"

"I used to be a policewoman myself."

"Then you know all about our high standards."

The inspector opened a window and traffic noise blasted into the room on a wave of hot air. "Here I wanted to treat you to some fresh air," the inspector apologised. "Bad idea." He closed the window again and sat down behind his desk.

"Yes, we've been through the traffic to get here. I don't need any more of it," Lerato sighed.

"Don't I know it." The inspector picked up a cardboard file from a pile on the floor. "Excuse the mess in here. We are drowning in work. It's not easy to make this case a priority."

"I know and we appreciate your cooperation. Which is more than can be said for our suspects." Lerato's mood softened. "So what have you got for us? We spoke to them this morning. So far all we got was hot air, rudeness and a few lies for good measure."

"You don't say… oops, I nearly forgot the coffee I promised you." Inspector Vorster left the office and came back five minutes later with two Styrofoam cups.

He made space on his desk and put the cups down. "I hope you like your coffee with milk and sugar. Makes it more tolerable, I think."

"That's fine, thank you," Charlie said. She didn't want to get into the hoo-ha of explaining insulin-resistance to him.

"I'm actually glad you're getting involved, Ms Gwala. I have my hands full as it is, even without these high-profile cases. If it wasn't for the Police Commissioner…"

"And here we thought you might feel that we are treading on your toes," Lerato said. Charlie was surprised how straight forward Lerato was with the policeman. But then, Lerato had been in the police force herself and knew the etiquette.

"No, not at all. Here, this is what we have so far. I sent you some of the crime scene photos and the suspects' pictures didn't I?"

"You did, inspector."

Marius Vorster passed the case file across the table. "Ugly way to go."

Some cars downstairs hooted riotously, but Lerato didn't seem to care about the traffic anymore. She skimmed through the content of the folder. It contained references, notes, the original reports and more photographs. The two sleuths studied everything carefully, asking questions here and there.

"I understand that Prof. de Vries would love to wrap up this case by the end of the month. That's apparently why he hired our agency," Lerato said.

"Ho! Wishful thinking. By the end of the month, hey?" He grinned. "But you never know. Miracles do happen."

"Yes, but as you said: you never know. He seems a bit cagey to us. Doesn't know much about his staff. Did you have the same impression?" Lerato put the file down next to her untouched coffee cup.

"Two of my officers went to speak to de Vries, because I was busy with another case. Arson, two dead. So I can't tell you much about it. Barely had time to look at the file. He's the only witness we saw."

He grabbed another cardboard file and pulled out a sheet of paper. "Here, the statement by Professor Deon de Vries." He handed Lerato the statement.

"Thank you for your confidence in us, Inspector Vorster."

"As I said, I'm grateful for the appointment of your agency. Many hands make light work. As long as we keep each other informed, I can see no problems. For starters, I could introduce you to my colleagues, who spoke to Prof. de Vries."

"Thank you that would be helpful. Then we could compare notes."

"We haven't spoken to any of the other witnesses or suspects, yet," the inspector added. "My boss informed me shortly after I was given the case that your agency would be taking over the interviews. So hooray for that."

He picked up the phone and not much later, two policemen in plainclothes entered the room. Inspector

Vorster introduced them and together, they discussed the statement with the help of the notes that Charlie had taken during the day. It was a short meeting and the policemen left 30 minutes later.

"I can see why you think they are ducking and diving," the inspector said after closing the door behind them. "Dr. Sibanda and the student who found the body…"

"Irina Lotcombe," Lerato said.

"Yes, that one… we should schedule follow-ups with them…"

"I was saying the same thing earlier," Lerato agreed.

Charlie pointed to one of the crime scene photos. "Is that a bloodied shoe print?"

The photo showed the outline of a sturdy sole in the dirt. The inspector smiled at her attentively and took the photograph she was holding.

"Hmm, it's a boot print, judging by the sole. But I can't say why there seems to be blood on it. It would indicate that somebody stepped into the blood on the ground. That could have a number of reasons."

"Why wasn't the boot print marked?" Lerato asked. "It's hard to tell what size it is."

"That's a good question," Inspector Vorster answered. "I'm afraid the crime scene wasn't secured very well. But then again, they don't get many homicides in the Kruger Park."

"We should check the crime scene out – or whatever's left of it as soon as possible," Lerato suggested and Charlie nodded.

"Right. Perhaps we should all go, to cover our bases. I would have to clear it with my superiors, but I could possibly accompany you."

"Are you sure? You said you were snowed under with work," Charlie said.

"Like it or not, this case ended up on my desk, so let's do things properly. My superiors won't like it, but for the Police Commissioner, they might make an exception." The inspector smiled at her.

"If you say so... we don't know how many animals have made their way through the area by now or if the wind has taken clues with it, but better now than never."

Charlie studied the photographs one by one again. She wondered what this Professor Morton could have done to end up in the Kruger Park with his brains bashed in.

"I'd appreciate that. We've spoken to the suspects in Joburg, so we could make ourselves available anytime," Lerato said and asked for a glass of water.

"Sure. The coffee not to your liking?"

"If this coffee is barely drinkable hot, then it probably tastes like dishwater when it's cold... just speaking from experience."

"I don't blame you. Water coming up." The inspector went outside and came back with two Styrofoam cups from the water cooler in the passage.

"Thank you." Lerato took the cups and handed one to Charlie.

"There is nothing in the report about anybody else being in the area at the time of the killing." Charlie took a sip of water. "So chances are slim that somebody might have seen anything."

"Hmm, we can check with the police officers in Hoedspruit. One more reason to go there," Inspector Vorster said and blushed a little when he looked at Charlie.

She sipped her water and noticed a calendar from 2017on the wall next to a whiteboard, scrawled all over with mind maps.

"Could you speak to your superiors, please?" Lerato asked. "The sooner we can move on this, the better." She felt impatient. They should get out of town before the start of the afternoon rush hour.

"Let me phone the superintendent right now. Let's see what he says."

He picked up the phone and dialled an in-house extension. 'Yes, hi Simphiwe, it's me, Marius. Do we have anything urgent on the next two days? Yes, I know, David can take over for a few days. It's about the case in the Kruger Park. The high-profile case. Yes, I know…. the police commissioner said to support the private detectives… they are here in my office. We need to have a look at the crime scene if nothing else. It'll only be a short trip to the Kruger. Two days max. Yes, Thursday, Friday? Thursday's tomorrow.' He checked his desk calendar. 'Okay, I'll tell them. Thank you. Yes, I will. See you later.' The two women looked at each other in anticipation.

"That sounded promising," Lerato said.

"I've been given permission by the superintendent to go on a fact-finding expedition with you. Tomorrow."

"Tomorrow? Well… why not? That's unexpectedly fast for the SAPS."

"The commissioner's word counts for something around here. I suppose my superiors try to please him. I'll make arrangements with them just now. We could drive up, see what we can find out, sleep over in Hoedspruit and come back."

"What about following up with Irina Lotcombe and Duncey?"

"It can wait until we come back."

"Then we better get going." Lerato stood up.

They shook hands. "I'll take care of the nitty-gritty and be in touch," he said.

His cell phone rang. The tune was Horse with No Name. 'Yes, yes, I do…' he answered the phone and stepped outside. Charlie and Lerato discussed the picture with the boot print until he came back inside.

"My partner, Inspector Johan Phaladi," he explained. "He's asking if you parked in his spot. A red Polo? Could you please move your car to the visitors' section?"

"Oh? Sorry about that," Lerato said innocently. "We were on our way in any case. For the record…

where is the visitors' section?" Lerato wanted to know. "We'll have to come back here one of these days."

"Well, you must drive past the staff section – that's where you parked - and then carry on straight. The visitors' parking is on the left-hand side at the back."

"I should find it next time around. Sorry."

"No worries. Could you give me the address where I must pick you up tomorrow morning?"

Lerato scribbled her details down. "Here…"

"Thank you Ms Gwala. Ms Proudfoot. We'll speak later, then."

Traffic was picking up as they made their way out of town. Lerato swore a lot in Xhosa and hooted at the odd driver. "I hate this traffic and it's getting dark! I hope we don't have to come back anytime soon… not bad, that inspector-guy," she said without skipping a beat.

"You think? Why did he smile at me all the time?" Charlie wondered. "Was it just me or did it seem a little…"

"Weird?" Lerato completed her friend's sentence and grinned.

"Yes. What's there to smile about?" Charlie asked. "Homicide's not exactly funny."

Lerato concentrated on the traffic and avoided pedestrians more than once. Many were waiting in queues at taxi ranks and walked into the street without looking. "Bloody hell! Watch where you are going! Maybe he likes you. Masendako!"

She grunted in frustration and swerved around a recycling collector who pulled a cart, heaped with large sacks full of plastic and glass bottles.

"No, I don't think so," Charlie replied calmly.

"I do..." Lerato flipped somebody off and found a gap ahead. Soon, they were on the city highway, heading north.

"Oh please, all I want to do is help you solve this case... I'm not interested. If he wants us to go to the Kruger Park in the morning, I need to organise the dogs, somehow. Jono is still in Durban. His friend's wedding is this weekend."

"I could ask someone to house sit for you," Lerato offered.

"Like who?"

"My boyfriend..." Lerato said as they drove under the flyover, past the city centre.

"Really, you have a boyfriend?!" Charlie was stunned.

"Didn't I tell you?"

"No, you didn't. You sly woman, holding out on me like that!" Charlie pinched her friend's arm.

"Ouch… It's all fairly new, but I'm sure you'll like him when you meet him. And he likes dogs. So everything's sorted," Lerato said as if it was all no problem at all.

"You haven't even asked him yet."

"I know he'll help out. He did house sitting when he was a student. And he'll do it for me." Lerato relaxed more and more as they left the city behind.

"You mean he would sleep over at my house and look after the dogs like a proper house sitter?" Charlie asked.

"Yes, what else?" Lerato looked at Charlie for a moment.

"But I don't even know him."

"Then I'll have to introduce the two of you, won't I?"

Finally, traffic was flowing again as they took the onramp to the highway. They didn't speak until they had left the M2 behind. "Man, am I glad we are out of the city!" Lerato groaned.

"You want to introduce us like now?" Charlie asked when traffic slowed down and came to a halt.

"There is no time like now. I'll ask him. Is it okay if he comes to meet us at your house? He should be off work by now. Give me my phone – it's in the handbag. I'll text him quickly." Charlie dug around in Lerato's handbag and gave her the phone.

"I don't even know his name," Charlie grumbled.

"His name is Peter Munirwa. He's a chartered accountant with Hepstone and Dladla. Good-looking and the nicest guy you can imagine." She typed a message and handed the phone back to Charlie when traffic started flowing again.

"What? An accountant? When did this happen?"

"Oh, a couple of months ago. I met him through a group of friends at a birthday party. Most of them were accountants. We had a real connection right from the start."

"A couple of months ago? I didn't know that you knew so many accountants."

"They are my half-sister's friends. She's an accountant at KWY, you know."

"No I didn't, but now I do."

"Peter is a nice guy," Lerato gushed. "Not like other accountants I've met. And he doesn't even drink, can you believe it?"

"Wow, any reason for that?"

"His Dad was an alcoholic, so he vowed never to touch hard drink. Just a glass of wine or a beer now and again if there is something to celebrate."

"He's got character, this Peter. Hope he doesn't celebrate too often." Lerato shot Charlie a withering look. "No seriously, I'm glad to see you so happy," Charlie said quickly. "I can't wait to meet this too-good-to be-true man."

"Oh, he's true enough and I'm really happy with him. We'll check his message when we get to your house."

"Let's check now."

Charlie looked up the message Peter Munirwa had sent. "He says you must let him know when we get home then he'll be there asap. That's very flexible of him. I can't believe that you were holding out on me you minx…"

They giggled and drove to Charlie's house. Sure enough, Lerato's new boyfriend arrived a few minutes later. Lerato had told her the truth: Peter was not only easy on the eye. Charlie noticed immediately that he was an intelligent and pleasant fellow, and

Lerato was bursting with pride. Peter got out of his car in the driveway and embraced his beaming girlfriend.

"It's so nice to meet you, Peter," Charlie greeted him. "I can't believe that Lerato has never told me about you until today."

"She hasn't?" He mock-scolded Lerato.

"I was going to tell her and in any case, you are here now. So simmer down people. Let's go sit down and meet properly," Lerato said firmly.

"We can sit outside until it gets dark," Charlie suggested and walked towards the kitchen gate. "It's still warm outside. Should I let the dogs out to meet you?"

"If you don't mind," Peter said. "I'd love to meet them."

Lerato and Peter sat down on plastic chairs in the back garden as Billie and Popcorn stormed out and danced around his legs. He petted their heads and talked to them as if he'd known the dogs forever.

"You're hired," Charlie laughed. "I'm really glad my friend here has a good taste in men. You're rather nice for an accountant and thanks for being so flexible."

"We need to go to the bush and it just can't wait," Lerato said.

"My warrior-woman," Peter joked and kissed her lightly on the lips. "You'll solve this case in no time."

Colin and Charlie had larked around just like that when they'd first met. She could just see his smiling face in front of her.

"Coffee or tea, anyone?" She asked quickly.

"Do you have hot chocolate?" Peter asked charmingly.

Charlie prepared three mugs in the kitchen and carried them outside. "Hot chocolate for the two of you. Thank you, by the way, for helping me out, Peter."

The dogs settled down under the table. "Anything for my lovely lady and her friend. And I truly love dogs. I just hope they will love me back."

"I don't see why not." Charlie smiled. "You've won them over already."

"Then it's sorted. I'll leave work a little earlier tomorrow afternoon and spend some time with your pooches in the garden. Do they have toys?"

"Yes, they do, but only Billie likes to play fetch. We have a new fire pit at the back of the garden if you want to use it. There are wood logs in the tub under the roof. Popcorn is a bit scared of flames, but he's fine as soon as the fire has died down."

The little white poodle got all excited when he heard his name and Billie began to dance around on her hind legs.

"Billie, down! Down. Where is your ball?" Charlie said and the dog brought a stick that was a few sizes too big for her.

"Sounds great to me, but I'm more of a dinner-in-front-of-the-TV kind of guy," Peter said and threw the stick onto the lawn.

Lerato nodded. "We can have a braai to celebrate the successful conclusion of our case. Here around your fire pit."

"Sure, that's a good idea," Charlie agreed. "Then you can meet my brother Jono as well, Peter. Provided we solve the case…"

"Of course we will!" Lerato insisted.

"There is no doubt in my mind that you will," Peter Munirwa said with an admiring look on his face and threw the stick again.

"Would you two like to stay for dinner? I'm going to make something quick like scrambled eggs."

"I'm afraid I'll have some packing to do," Lerato told Charlie. "The inspector just phoned when you were inside. He'll pick me up and then we'll come to you at about 6:30 in the morning. So we haven't got much time to prepare. Don't forget your hat and sun lotion."

"And my toothbrush. I guess we'll sleep at a guesthouse in Hoedspruit. It's a bit far to come back the same day."

"Everything's organised. Our good inspector's on the ball. Alright then, drink up kids. We have work to do."

When Lerato and Peter were leaving, Billie and Popcorn ran ahead to the front gate and barked. Charlie whistled and there was a deep growl outside that grew into a wild bark, then another one.

The hairstylist from across the road was walking her dogs without a leash in the dark. She didn't take any notice of the three people standing by the gate. Charlie yanked the gate closed and tried to stop her two little yappers from barking back at them.

The woman could barely control her barking dogs and a car came to a screeching halt in front of her. The woman swore at the puzzled driver and walked on as if nothing was wrong.

"What the hell…" Lerato said. "What's wrong with these new neighbours of yours? It's against the law to walk your dog in the street without a leash. She's lucky I'm no longer in the force."

"The old lady is even more annoying. Some days, she stands in front of our driveway for a while, just to rile the dogs up." Charlie shook her head.

Peter glanced from Lerato to Charlie. "Are you having neighbour trouble?" He wanted to know and Charlie explained the situation in a nutshell. "Unfortunately. Please make sure to lock them up before you leave for work in the morning."

"I'll remember that. Some people…" Peter said and pressed his car remote control. Beep. Beep.

"Bye, hunn. I'll see you tomorrow morning bright and early." Lerato hugged Charlie. "Remember…. sunhat, sun lotion and your toothbrush!"

"I'll be there and ready for action, sunhat and all."

That night, Charlie had a disturbing dream about earrings. Long earrings with red stones like drops of blood.

Chapter FIVE

The off-road vehicle bounced along at high speed. Inspector Vorster sat on the passenger seat. He had taken off his suit jacket and wiped his brow. He'd forgotten how much warmer the Kruger Park was than the city on the Highveld.

Charlie and Lerato held onto the seats in front of them with both hands, while being jostled around on the backseat. A cloud of swirling dust trailed the car and a warm wind blasted the passengers mercilessly. They were on their way to the crime scene, where Professor Morton's body had been found just days before.

They had a full programme. After a long drive to Hoedspruit, they had dropped off their things at the guesthouse and met Sergeant Mokhodi at the local police station.

He now steered the car confidently along the bumpy road and tried to answer their questions. Ever since they'd passed the gate into the park and left the tarred road, his answers were barely audible. The conversation sounded like whispering between Inspector Vorster and Sergeant Mokhodi.

Lerato was holding the map in her left hand. "Isn't the camp in that direction down there?" She yelled. The vehicle jumped over a dip in the road and swayed a little.

"We're going first to the crime scene," Sergeant Mokhodi yelled back and waved to his left. "We'll stop by the camp later."

"Okay, I see." Lerato put the map on her lap.

Charlie sat between Lerato and one of the rangers, who often worked with the scientists. It was part of his job to keep an eye on the wild dogs and report to the zoologists on a regular basis. Charlie couldn't remember the man's name. Alan… something. He didn't seem to mind the potholes and evasive turns around random rocks, and he was quite chatty.

"The dogs move for all sorts of reasons, but never very far from their original den," the ranger said to Charlie. He didn't have to yell. His voice was sonorous and carried over the noise in the car, despite his strong Afrikaans accent. Charlie nodded and looked at Lerato, but her friend wasn't paying attention to the ranger and kept staring out the window. A few springboks zig-zagged across the dry grass.

"The professor was a friendly man. Always thanked me for my cooperation. I enjoyed working with him." The ranger adjusted his hat and changed the subject.

"Bliksem! That something so horrible should take place in the Kruger! Everybody around here is still spooked by the murder. Our next group of volunteer rangers is coming in a few days. I'll have to explain it to them what happened." The ranger seemed rattled. "Never in my 18 years as a ranger for SafParks has anything like this happened..." The police vehicle kept bounding along the rough ground.

Inspector Vorster replied something, but Charlie could not understand what he said. Sergeant Mokhodi turned halfway around, keeping his eyes on the road.

"We're almost there," he informed them. As they approached the site by the slope, Charlie could see the dusty tops of thorn trees.

"Over there, behind the trees is the new den of the pack." Alan, the ranger said. "Prof. Morton spotted them on the night, he died. We found his notes."

The policeman nodded and turned to the left. Ten

minutes later, they stopped close to the edge of the slope. The inspector got out first with wobbly legs.

"So, this is where it happened, then," Lerato stated the obvious.

The two women were glad to get their feet on solid ground and breathed in the unique scent of the savannah. Inspector Vorster looked flushed and sweaty, his white shirt no longer fresh. It was just past lunchtime and their sunhats came in handy in the bright sun.

"Sorry we had to go so fast," the ranger apologised. "If you drive slowly, the car might get stuck in the sandy bits." He waved for them to follow. "Over here, see? That's where we found him."

He pointed to a spot on the slope where the dirt was still disturbed. Brownish patches indicated where the body had come to rest. They walked down the narrow path to get closer to the spot.

"Prof was found here head-down. The monitoring equipment was by the treeline in a small tent."

Sergeant Mokhodi balanced across to the bloody patches and the others followed him. Some of the bloodied grit had slid down when the police had taken the body away. "The coroner says he had a sprained ankle. The boot was tied to his belt. He had also some bruising on his thigh and shin and probably sustained them in a fall hours before. They were unrelated to the head wounds that killed him. You probably know that there were no defensive wounds. We assumed that he was either asleep or caught by surprise."

"It's difficult to reconstruct what happened here," Inspector Vorster said. "The victim might have faced away from the killer."

"Yes. He bled out here." The policeman pointed to the ground. "We suspect that the murder weapon was a heavy object with a disk-like feature. I had my men comb the area and the woods down there, but there was no trace of a possible weapon. Killer must have taken it with him. We secured tyre marks up there that are different from the researchers' vehicles or ours. It's all in the report. They come from a Hilux. Very common for bakkies here. Most of the farmers drive a Hilux. We did some comparisons, but no match as yet."

"Are you saying that the killers aren't local?" Marius Vorster asked.

"It's unlikely in any case. The locals have no issues with the researchers. There is no motive for murder as far as I can tell." The ranger took off his hat and wiped his forehead. Sergeant Mokhodi was quick to back him up. "We have no suspects from around here."

"Unlikely or not, we would need a list from you," the inspector insisted. "Perhaps we have witnesses. Were there any tourists in the area or any locals for that matter?"

"Hard to tell. There are a few timeshares closer to the gate. We are still looking into it. And the tourist camps are fully booked at any point in time."

Charlie saw a few meerkats standing upright above their burrow, watching the human intruders. They hurried underground when the ranger began to speak.

"I could have a chat with the camp managers," he offered. "I'll e-mail you the information when I get it." He nodded to the police sergeant.

The inspector thanked him. "Good. Perhaps we have witnesses, after all."

"It's not exactly the centre of Hoedspruit, but you never know," the sergeant said.

They plodded back up the slope, while Charlie ambled down the path towards the trees, avoiding sharp stones spiking up from the ground. She poked with a stick here and there and squatted down every so often to look at something more closely. The ranger followed her with his eyes.

Inspector Vorster noticed white splashes on the ground outlining a long rectangle. "I see that you've taken casts of the tyre marks."

"Yes, the tracks on this side were made in softer soil, so we managed to get clear imprints." The sergeant was clearly proud that the police had done their job, although the inspector could be so critical.

"Did you analyse the matter inside the tyre marks?" Lerato asked.

"Like what?" The police officer asked gruffly. He wondered what these women were doing here, anyway. Everything was well in hand.

"There might be plant matter or a different type of soil present. It could indicate a location where the vehicle's been before."

"We are not that sophisticated around here, but you are welcome to take samples."

"Thank you, sergeant. We should also inspect the casts," Lerato said. "I suppose they are still at the police station."

"Yes, they are. I'll sign them out to you."

"Where is the boot print on the photograph?" Inspector Vorster studied the picture in his hand and compared it to the ground.

"Over there," the policeman pointed to a spot on top of the slope. The faint outline of a print was still visible.

"It's a larger size from what I can see," he said. "Definitely a man."

"Or a woman with extraordinarily large feet," Lerato grinned and the inspector grinned back.

"Or that…let me take a few pictures of it."

The inspector used his cell phone again to add photographs of the boot print to the assortment of pictures he had taken on the rise. The inspector put his watch down for comparison and snapped away. "The red soil is darker in places. It could have looked like blood on the crime scene pictures."

"So we can write that one off," Lerato said. "Let's assume that it was a man, did you measure the size? Did you compare the tread to the professor's boots?" Lerato peppered the questions at Sergeant Mokhodi. "And do we know the shoe sizes of our current suspects?"

"No Ma'am," the policeman said, visibly embarrassed at not having noted down the shoe sizes. "We hadn't thought of that."

"Then let's measure the print before it completely disappears." She took out a measuring tape and held it against the soil next to the boot print. "I'd say it's a size 11 boot. So it was definitely a man. We can't be sure that it was the killer, though. The tread is not distinct." She scratched around between the stones. "I also don't think that's blood, but we'll take a sample, just to be sure. What size was the professor's boot?"

The sergeant and the ranger looked at each other. "Prof had large feet," Alan said.

Sergeant Mokhodi paged through his paperwork. "Here it is. For a moment I thought we didn't put that information in. A size 11."

"Wouldn't be surprised," Lerato mumbled to herself. "So it's likely that Professor Morton himself made the boot print," she said aloud.

"Good thing we came to have a look at the scene," the inspector mused. "Keeps us from chasing off in the wrong direction. If there's no blood and the victim made the print himself, the evidence is useless."

The police sergeant looked stumped. "I guess it would be. But we still have the tyre cast."

Lerato looked around. "The tyre tracks over here have a lighter soil in them. They haven't been cast. Any reason why?"

"I think it was an oversight," Sergeant Mokhodi sounded embarrassed. "There were so many vehicles up here after the body was found."

"Hmm. Where would we find this lighter coloured soil, then?" Lerato asked.

"I'd say there's lighter soil more towards Hoedspruit," the ranger answered. "But that proves nothing."

"Didn't you say that the timeshares are closer to the gate?"

"I did. If one of the people there were up here, we'd be wasting our time, checking the tyres of bakkies in the area," the police sergeant said.

"We also can't assume that the two scientists, who found the professor, arrived after the murder had been committed, either," Lerato said. "But we have to start somewhere. I'll take a cast. There's no time like now."

She proceeded to mix a bag of plaster with water from a canister she had brought in a large shopping bag together with other tools of the trade.

"You came prepared, lady. Here' I'll help you," the ranger offered and stirred the mixture until it was smooth, then poured it into the tracks.

There was an uneasy silence as they waited for the cast to set, accompanied by perpetual bird song and occasional yelping from beyond the wood. Finally, she lifted the hardened cast, wrapped it in plastic and put it in the back of the police vehicle.

"It's just a theory, but what if somebody planned the murder for whatever reason and knew where the professor was at that time?" Lerato pondered.

"That's possible but unlikely," Alan said.

"Oh? And why is it unlikely?" Lerato wanted to know.

"Because when the team left Joburg, they didn't even know where the wild dogs would be taking their pups. That's what they were busy monitoring. Prof could easily have been somewhere else."

"So, how would a killer - who is not familiar with this information and is not acquainted with the area - know where to look for the victim?"

"How indeed," the inspector muttered. "An insider, then? One of the team?"

"Or somebody, who was in contact with the team… but then we'd need motive."

"And proof," Inspector Vorster reminded her.

"If there was internet reception around here, perhaps, but even in Hoedspruit Wi-Fi is sketchy at best," the ranger answered.

"But not impossible." Lerato began to debate possible scenarios in her mind.

"No, not impossible," he agreed.

While they were deliberating next to the vehicle, Charlie was still at the foot of the slope. She bent down and picked something up that had caught her eye. Something that did not belong in the dirt.

She turned the small object over in her hand and wondered what she was looking at. Something round made of plastic and a bit of metal in the middle. She scanned the ground, but there was nothing else of interest to her. Charlie made her way up the path to present her find to Lerato and the inspector.

"Looks like part of an earring. The back piece that holds it in place. I think it's called a butterfly," Lerato said and Marius Vorster bagged the evidence.

He had brought his own supply of small sandwich

bags that came in handy at crime scenes.

"Isn't it a bit odd that the equipment was picked up down there on the same night by the team? The ones that found him, according to the police report," Charlie mused. "How could they have known where to look?"

"Why?" Lerato asked. "The student told us that Dr. Sibanda used the torchlight to search the area. After they'd found the body."

"Oh yes, that's right. Odd thing to look for their equipment at a time like this."

"I suppose they saw that it wasn't in the jeep. But you're right; it was pitch dark that night at about 10 past eight. I remember that the time was mentioned in the report," the inspector said. Lerato looked surprised.

"Yes, I did read the report last night," he confirmed. "And saw the photo with the little tent and all."

"Maybe they tried to see if somebody was there. Then saw the tent next to the footpath by chance," Lerato offered an explanation.

"I don't think so. Apparently, it was behind those bushes and rocks almost by the trees." Marius Vorster shook his head.

"Maybe the tent reflected the light?"

"Let me see that picture again." Lerato studied the photograph of the tent in the dark. "You're right, Charlie. There are reflective stripes on the tent."

"That leads us back to the woman with the earring." The inspector mused.

"What's the conclusion? That a woman was with the victim, fought with him, chased him up the slope and killed him with a heavy object?"

"No, that doesn't sound likely," Inspector Vorster said. "All the female researchers were accounted for. Is it possible that the crime scene was contaminated?" asked.

"By whom? There's virtually nobody around at night. My men don't wear earrings," Sergeant Mokhodi answered. "There were no female police officers around to secure the crime scene, either."

"I bet," Lerato couldn't help a sarcastic remark that was lost on the men. "How do you think, this butterfly made its way down there?"

"I wouldn't know," the inspector said. "We'll look around a bit more, but a woman likely lost that butterfly during the night to pick up the things the victim left bchind when he tried to get up there to his car."

"And that woman was... the grad student?"

Charlie said. "Dr. Naidoo doesn't have pierced ears.

They walked down and searched together where Charlie had found the butterfly.

"I think I got something." Lerato held up a long earring with red teardrop-shaped stones in her gloved hand. "It was sticking out a little from under that rock. it must have rolled down the side of the slope." Charlie was stunned. She had dreamed about this earring. The question was when had it been lost?

"Look what we have here." The inspector wiped his forehead.

"Now we just need to establish the owner," Sergeant Mokhodi said. " I wonder why my men found nothing down there during the search."

Inspector Vorster picked up the earring with a tissue before dropping it into one of his clear sandwich bags. "You tell me…"

"It's still not hard evidence, but at least we have something." Lerato shrugged her shoulders. "We should go and investigate the campsite."

"Yes, perhaps we'll find some clues there," Marius Vorster agreed.

On their way up, Charlie saw the meerkats again.

The little mongooses were observing them suspiciously. If you could only talk, she thought.

"I suppose the wild dogs are too far away for us to sneak a look at, Alan?" Charlie asked the ranger.

"We shouldn't disturb them, while they are denning. That's what the monitoring equipment is used for. We have binoculars to observe them from elevated points and only upwind. They are shy animals and for good reason. Humans are seen as predators, I'm afraid."

"We could look at them through your binoculars…"

"We won't have time for a safari today, Ms Proudfoot," the inspector said good-naturedly. "We need to get going." He looked uncomfortable, which was hardly surprising in this heat.

"We should go, then."

"Maybe I'll take you on a safari some other time. Just let me know when you want to come." The ranger gave Charlie an inviting smile. "But speaking about predators…" He pointed to one of the trees.

"Oh my goodness! That's so amazing." Charlie's jaw dropped. The others turned around. "What is it?" Lerato strained her eyes.

"There's a leopard in that tree over there! Right on top. You can see him with the naked eye. I think he's got a gazelle with him," Charlie marvelled.

"Wow! Such a little gazelle," Lerato said with a touch of sadness.

"Well, even leopards have to eat."

Everybody had a good look before climbing into the back of the police vehicle. Charlie found herself squashed between the inspector and Lerato, this time. Lerato held the plaster cast between her knees, to keep it from getting damaged.

Charlie took off her hat and saw a giraffe standing stock-still in the bush. The animal was well-camouflaged and almost invisible between the dust-covered trees and shrubs.

She nudged Lerato, but the giraffe had disappeared. The ranger sat in the front, holding onto the side of the window frame and chatted to the police sergeant in Afrikaans. He'd probably seen thousands of those graceful animals.

Although they were here to solve a murder, Charlie couldn't help but be moved. She had spotted meerkats, a leopard and a giraffe in the Kruger Park.

It took them a few minutes to get to the campsite. It consisted of permanent tents, arranged in a semi-circle. Iron pots and various camping implements were stored in the supply tent, closest to the fireplace. It was unlocked. Nobody had ever tried to steal supplies.

"Whoever stays at the site brings their own food, water, petrol and special equipment," the ranger explained. "We also use it for training new rangers. The local police keep an eye on it, but it's quite safe. Isn't it, Lucas?"

"Yes, quite safe," Sergeant Mokhodi agreed.

They opened the next tent to look inside. There were four narrow bed frames, blankets, camp chairs and tables. The other tents were virtually identical.

"They used two of the tents. This is where Professor Morton and the other two men slept. And that one over there is the women's tent."

"Where do you sleep?" Lerato asked the broad-shouldered ranger.

"I have a house in town."

"So you go home every day?"

"Yes."

"Where do you have your office?"

"At my house. We have meetings in my lounge or I come out to the campsite with my assistants. Usually, we're gone by nightfall unless we are needed."

"So you weren't around when Professor Morton left the camp to monitor the dogs that afternoon?" The inspector picked up the thread.

"No, I went to my daughter's birthday party. Ellie. She turned 6 on Friday, and there was no need for me to hang around until late. I was called out later by Lucas."

Charlie took a look at the tent that was used to store provisions. Cool drink cartons were neatly stacked on top of each other with plastic boxes on either side.

She shuddered. A large rain spider was stretching its legs on the inner sheet of the roof not far from her. After a paralysing second, Charlie Proudfoot beat a hasty retreat. Spiders were to be expected in the wild, but she hated the mere sight of them.

Unfortunately, hunting spiders like this one were not exactly rare in the city either. It was Jono's job to take them out of the house. Once, she'd tried to pin a baboon spider to the floor with a book, but the spider had walked towards her, book and all. Ugh.

The ranger and Sergeant Mokhodi scratched around in the cold ashes of the fireplace, while Lerato and the inspector searched the other tents, then the ground outside, but they found nothing of interest.

"Do you remember anything unusual on that day?" Marius Vorster directed the question at Alan.

"Such as?" The ranger asked in a surprised tone and Charlie had the feeling, he wasn't going to tell them the truth.

"Anything that could explain the murder."

"Not that I could pick up on anything. Although Prof. Morton seemed a little impatient that day."

"Why would you say that?" Lerato probed.

"Usually, he's more relaxed. But that day, he seemed kind of … nervous."

"Nervous? Any particular reason why he should be nervous?"

"I didn't ask him. When people live together for a couple of weeks, all sorts of things can happen. I didn't stay long, because of my daughter's party."

"Has anything…unpleasant ever happened during such a research trip?"

"Rarely," Alan said. "Well, we had a bit of a

situation sometime back when Professor de Vries stayed here with his girlfriend and three volunteers. I think the girlfriend was hot on one of the volunteers or something. I don't remember clearly. And last year, two ladies didn't seem to like each other very much and had to share the tent with other volunteers. But as I said that sort of thing doesn't normally happen."

"So Professor de Vries is also taking trips to the Kruger Park? I didn't know he was involved in wild dog conservation," Lerato replied.

The inspector puffed out his cheeks. At last, the sun was sinking and a breeze cooled him down.

"He isn't. Wild dogs were Professor Morton's thing. De Vries was checking up on our rhinos," the ranger clarified.

"I see. Do you remember the names of these women or Prof. de Vries's girlfriend, perhaps?" Lerato asked him. This was taking an interesting turn.

"The girlfriend's name was Cheryl or Cherie, I think, and the volunteers are usually APE students from some university. The one woman last year was called Karin something. Sorry, I'm not very good with names," the ranger rambled a little.

"Right." Lerato and the inspector were taking notes, while Charlie followed a hunch and took another look at the supply tent.

"What do we have here…" She pulled something shiny out from between two cool drink boxes. "Now that's interesting."

*

"Okay yes, we did bring back the equipment and the tent when Prof was lying on the slope. I saw the reflectors behind some bushes. I knew that the equipment had to be around somewhere. We couldn't just leave it behind. There was also his camera. I checked the pictures, but there were just wild dogs and three of …"

"Miss Lotcombe…" the inspector tried to stop her flow of words. "We asked you a simple question: Is this your earring?"

"… the leopard. And yes, it's my earring. I must have lost it when I picked something up. What's wrong with it?"

Lerato Gwala, Marius Vorster and Charlie Proudfoot had just begun to question the student in the Dean's meeting room at the university. They had come straight from the Kruger Park to the university.

Luckily Irina Lotcombe had been busy with some paperwork, but she seemed frazzled. Today, even the routine questions threw her off. At least, there were no more tears.

"Astonishing that you had the wherewithal to collect the equipment that night. Finding a dead body must have been a great shock to you," Lerato probed.

"It was... of course it was, but as I said, we couldn't just leave everything behind. The stuff is expensive." The white of her eyes was showing. A clear sign that she wasn't telling them the whole truth.

"Right. Why didn't you tell the police about this?" The inspector asked.

"I thought I did."

"It wasn't in the report the police in Hoedspruit gave us," Charlie said.

"That's hardly my fault." Irina Lotcombe rolled her eyes. "I had the feeling that policewoman wasn't paying attention to what I was saying. So yes, I did tell her about the equipment. I'm sure of it." Irina looked even more flustered.

"I wonder what else the policewoman left out in her report. We were told that there were no female police officers around that night."

"No female officers?" The student's answer didn't sound convincing. "I thought it was a woman. I'm pretty sure it was a woman…"

"No, it wasn't. Do you mind if we ask you a few more questions?" Lerato asked in an insistent tone.

"Sure, why not?" Irina Lotcombe tried to sound easy-going, but Charlie didn't buy it. "I just have to supervise a tutorial in half an hour on Medical Campus."

"Then get somebody else to take over from you, please." The inspector's voice was stern. "Or send word that you won't be coming." He was unwilling to give up that easily when she was about to shed some light on the case.

"Sure." The student took out her cell phone and typed a message for one of the other tutors. "Hope he gets this in time. We are busy people, you know."

"I know, and we'll try to keep it brief. If you like, we can give you a ride to Medical Campus later."

"Thanks, I have my own car." Her cell phone pinged. "Ah okay. John says he can take over until I come." She sounded relieved.

"So let's get on with it then," Lerato said. "We

found one of your earrings at the crime scene and the other one in the supply tent at the camp. Can you tell us how you lost the second earring?"

"If I just knew… probably left the other one in the tent when we packed up. Stupid idea to take them with me to the camp. Not exactly practical." She tried to smile.

"Why did you take the earrings with you on that trip?" Lerato asked.

"I don't know. I guess I thought they were pretty."

"Did you want to be pretty in the Kruger Park?"

"Not exactly," the student mumbled and looked up to her left again.

"Right. Can you please tell us again what you did on the night of the murder? Let's start with the afternoon. You typed up the report when Professor Morton left to monitor the pack of dogs. Mr. Duncey confirms this, but Dr. Sibanda said that you went for a walkabout."

"Yes, I went to the latrine for a bit. You know… that time of the month."

"How long would you say did this trip to the latrine last?"

"Oh, I don't know… 20 minutes or more." The woman blushed and Charlie studied her face. "You know… it can take a while."

"You must have seen Mr. Duncey, then. Dr. Sibanda saw him leave camp in the same direction for some time. He was collecting plants'?"

"No, no I don't recall seeing him." She rolled strips of paper into tight little balls.

"Now, did Professor Morton seem… different to you that day?"

"Let me see…" Irina looked up to her right as if she could see the events of that day in front of her. "Not really. I mean it was Thokozo's turn to make dinner. He was busy with the food and I typed my report, as you know. I was waiting for Prof. We were going to leave for Joburg the following day, so it was the last chance to collect data I needed to complete the report. I think he enjoyed going on his own. Prof seemed fine to me."

"Not nervous?"

"Nervous? No, a bit excited maybe." She unrolled the paper balls one by one.

"So did you get the data?"

"Yes I did, it was in Prof's shirt pocket. The location of the new den for the next group and which animals were around the new den. He stopped recording the time at about ten past six."

"You took the notes out of his shirt pocket?" This time, the inspector asked the question.

"Yes, but that's all I took, I swear!"

"What happened before you went to look for the victim?"

"Dr. Naidoo was not in a good mood, so I tried to stay out of her way. Thokozo said we should eat without Prof. because he didn't answer his car radio. We thought Prof was still busy and Thokozo... I mean Dr. Sibanda kept some of the food for him. We didn't know..."

"What happened after dinner?"

"We took a drive to the location where we thought Prof might be, taking readings. And... we saw his car. Then we found him." She smiled sadly

"You mean you and Dr. Sibanda?"

The student nodded. "What went through your mind when you found the body?"

"He wasn't by the car, so we used our torches. First we thought he went for a pee, then Thokozo thought he hurt himself or something. We called his name but when we saw him lying head-down, we knew that he must be dead. It was a shock. Who thinks of such things when they work in wildlife conservation?"

"Nobody would think that."

"Exactly. Maybe the leopard got to him, Thokozo said. Then I found him and we saw that his head was bashed in. Brain tissue and… blood." Charlie thought she was getting sick, but then Irina stopped talking about the gory details.

"Do you remember the time when you found the victim?" Marius Vorster asked.

"It must have been after 7 o'clock or 8. It was already dark. Maybe we should have left sooner but we couldn't have known…"

"No, of course not. So what did you do?" The inspector asked.

"We… I think I must have screamed and… I mean he was just lying there with his shoes off and there was blood and he… I touched him. He was still warm, but he didn't breathe."

"Is that when you took the observation notes?"

"Yes. Then Thokozo radioed the camp and they called the police. I don't remember much of what happened afterwards."

"Did you at any stage hear or see anyone else or anything suspicious?"

"Something suspicious?"

"Did you have reason to believe that anybody else was around or had been there before you arrived?" The inspector clarified.

"No, I didn't… I don't know. But there must have been somebody earlier. The guy, who killed Prof."

"And witnesses, perhaps."

She looked confused. "I don't know. I wish I could help you, but I just don't know. Can I go now?"

"Yes, thank you for your time, Miss Lotcombe. Please keep yourself available and don't leave town. We might still have questions. Here is my card – in case you remember something important," Lerato gave her one of the new Maitirelo Agency cards that Florence had organised.

"Okay then, bye." The student left the room.

"Do you think, we should question the other suspects again?" Lerato asked the inspector. "Mr. Duncey and Dr. Sibanda. Their testimonies doesn't quite correspond."

"We could, but we still have to go through the lists and examine the casts."

"True. What do you think, Charlie?"

Her friend hadn't said a word while the inspector and Lerato questioned the student. "She is not telling the truth," Charlie told them.

"Why do you think that?" Lerato asked.

"Body language. And because of that feeling, I get from her. Almost as if she was angry. She had a hard time hiding something."

"You had a feeling?" The inspector asked in a condescending tone.

"Maybe I should explain, Marius," Lerato said. "Charlie here often has… what should I call it? Hunches… about people and situations and so on. She's usually right. Our agency is sometimes making use of her intuitive abilities."

"You're a psychic?"

"No, not exactly. I'd rather call it intuition or having hunches," Charlie answered.

"Really? The police force used to involve psychics at some stage, but they didn't have a lot of success with it. The case where a bunch of girls were kidnapped, for instance. The girls were never found."

"You don't have to believe in intuition," Lerato came to Charlie's defence. "We just follow up on her suggestions. If she says that the student is lying, then I'm convinced that there is something to it."

"I don't know anything about this case, but in the States, some police departments had great success with psychics. I'm not saying that I am a psychic, but my hunches can be helpful at times. Like now." Charlie felt uncomfortable explaining this.

"Alright then, glad we cleared that up," Marius Vorster chuckled. "Then let's have a look at the casts for now. I'm still waiting for the ranger to send me the names. Until he does, I'm sure we can squeeze in some questions."

Chapter SIX

"Is that it?" The taxi driver stopped outside the gate.

"Yes, that's the house."

A young man in a sports jacket and duffel bag paid the driver and opened the back door of the cab. He walked up to the gate and fumbled for the keys in his pocket. The lights were still on in the lounge, so he decided to go there first.

Shouldn't the dogs be here somewhere? He thought and took out a small bag with treats. He groped his way through the dark kitchen, past the table and along the passage.

He could hear that the TV was on and opened the lounge door. The dogs were on the smaller couch and growled at the sudden commotion. They had been snoozing to the white noise of a soap opera. Could this mean danger?

"It's just me," Jono said in a cheerful voice and the dogs started wincing with joy. He opened the door wide and got the fright of his life. Instead of his sister

Charlie, a strange man lay on the couch, waking up with a start from his nap. A large man.

It took Peter a moment before he realised that somebody was standing in the door. An intruder? This Peter hadn't expected. He jumped up. Was he in for a fight? Would the house be robbed on his watch?

"Who the hell are you?" Jono yelled confused and the man stared at him with a startled expression.

The dogs didn't bark. Strange that they tolerated an intruder.

"I could ask you the same thing!" Peter Munirwa shouted. He picked up the remote control and puffed out his chest. The unshaved young man was holding something. If this man had a weapon, he had no choice but to concede. There wasn't much he could do with a remote control.

"What're you doing here? This is not your house!" Jono didn't know what else to say. Peter was just as confused.

"I know that. I'm housesitting for Charlie." The dogs sniffed around Jono's legs and whimpered a little. Popcorn tried to lick his hand that was holding the small bag with treats and kept jumping up against his leg.

Jono needed a moment to digest the fact that a large man was on his sister's couch taking a nap with her dogs. He'd instinctively grabbed a candlestick by the door. Now he let it sink when he realised that the stranger didn't pose a threat. Jono put it back on the side table. It was a lot to take in, but thankfully he was not a hothead.

"You didn't plan on hitting me with that thing there, did you?" The large man said, sounding worried. He pointed the remote control at the candlestick on the side table by the door and Jono stepped away from it.

"Sorry, but I don't think we've met. Why are you housesitting? I thought I knew what my sister was up to, but obviously she didn't tell me that she had a new boyfriend," he said and pushed his hair back. It was all a bit much to take in.

"No, wait a minute… I'm not Charlie's boyfriend. If you're her brother, aren't you supposed to be in Durban at somebody's wedding? My name is Peter, by the way. Peter Munirwa."

Billie sensed that Jono was tense about their new

friend being in the house. She jumped onto the couch to show her support for Jono and started barking at Peter.

"It's alright, Billie." The men said in unison.

The little dog settled down and Jono gave the pooches their treats at last.

"Yes, I was in Durban. The bride stood my friend up at the altar that's why things ended early and I had to catch a lift back to Joburg. They dropped me off in Linksfield and I took a taxi from there. Long story short."

"Okay…"

"I couldn't get hold of my sister. Your name's Peter Munirwa you say? I'm sure I've never heard your name around here before. Maybe I should give Charlie a call and let her explain the whole thing to me."

Peter nodded his head and switched the TV off. "I'm Lerato's boyfriend."

"Lerato doesn't have a boyfriend," Jono said, still not satisfied with the answers he was getting.

"She does now. For the past two months to be precise. And I wouldn't try to phone Charlie," Peter said and Jono's suspicion returned.

"Oh, and why not?"

"They went to the Kruger Park to solve a murder case."

"A murder case? I thought she was done with that!"

"Apparently not. Lerato told me that a scientist was murdered and Charlie could help her with the case."

"The wild dog researcher? I heard about it on the news in the car."

"Yes, I think so. Look man, if you want me to leave, I don't mind. I was just doing her a favour by looking after the dogs tonight. They are supposed to come back tomorrow." Peter picked up the blanket that had slid onto the floor. "If you want me to leave, I can go…"

"No… no, it's okay. If Charlie says you can sleep here, you can stay, of course. But this is Joburg, Peter. You don't just come home to find a stranger sitting in the lounge. I thought you were an intruder."

"I get that… and I'm sorry, but I guess Charlie didn't have time to tell you. They left early this morning with some police inspector and nobody expected you back so soon." The two men sat down. "And I'm glad you don't mean me any harm!"

"I don't blame you. If she's in the Kruger, that explains why I couldn't get hold of her. They don't seem to have reception there, but she could have sent me at least a message…"

"Maybe she forgot or she thought it wasn't that urgent."

Charlie Proudfoot's brother saw the bottle of red wine on the couch table next to a bowl of salted peanuts. "Do you mind if I help myself to a glass of wine? I nearly had a heart attack when I saw you."

"Sure, help yourself. Wait, I'll get another glass from the cabinet."

"Thanks."

The two men chatted until Jono had finished his wine. "I'm off to bed," he said. "I stay in the cottage at the back."

"Well, it was good meeting you, Jono. I wish we had been introduced to each other before, but you're not half bad. Apart from wanting to smash my head in with a candlestick."

"No hard feelings, Peter. I'm beat after all that drama in Durban – and now this."

"I bet. Hope your friend Dave will get over his heartbreak soon. Not nice to be left standing at the altar like that."

"Yeah, bummer, but I'm sure he'll be okay. Went off to spend a week in their honeymoon suite and took a friend with. Too late to cancel the booking. You know where everything is, I'm sure. I'll take the dogs to the kitchen." Jono's attitude toward the stranger had changed completely, now that he'd met him properly. "Good night."

"Thanks, man." Before he switched the lights off in the guest bedroom, Peter set the alarm on his cell phone and typed a quick message.

As soon as his head hit the pillow, the young accountant was fast asleep.

*

Charlie had come home to find her brother at the house. She wasn't too surprised, because Lerato's boyfriend had sent her a brief message explaining the situation.

"So you've met our new house-sitter?" Charlie winked at Jono. They were having tea in the kitchen.

The dogs were lying peacefully in their baskets after a wild barking concert by the gate. The neighbour had taken her dogs to the park later than usual. Now Billie and Popcorn were watching the siblings, happy that they were both back.

"Yeah, I did. Do you have any idea how shocked I was to find a stranger in the house? Why didn't you send me a message or something?"

"I tried to phone you, but you didn't answer. And then I was in the bush. It all happened so quickly. That's why Peter was here. Nice of him to offer."

"Sorry I didn't answer my phone. I guess I was a little distracted after Dave's fiancée got cold feet and didn't even show up at the church. But Peter's a nice guy, so it's all good."

They spoke about the events that had unfolded during the wedding celebrations on the North Coast. Well, the almost-wedding celebrations.

"They had a fight before the big day. Something about Dave's ex showing up uninvited with her new boyfriend at the dinner. I mean that's not his fault."

"Yeah, bummer. How did his ex know about the dinner?"

"Social media, probably. Dave was recording everything on Instagram. Crazy lady, but the bride wasn't much better. So immature."

"How's Dave holding up?" Charlie wanted to know.

"He wasn't too happy when we left, but I just couldn't take it anymore. I mean why did he even want to marry that bimbo? It was nice to see the guys again after such a long time, though."

"To be honest, I barely remember Dave. Weren't you on the cricket team together?" Charlie asked.

"Yeah… the cricket team in grade 2."

"Oh, that's why I can't remember him. Didn't he tell you why he wanted to get married to what's her name?"

"Chanelle. Guys don't talk about stuff like that - generally. As I said, I hadn't seen him and the other guys for ages, so I didn't think he wanted to share that with me. I'd even bought a dark blue suit to go with the colour scheme and all. They'd paired me with this full-bodied blonde chick. The bridesmaids had to wear this purple colour to go with the flowers and we'd practised…"

"I'm sure you'll find another use for the suit," Charlie interrupted his flow of words.

"It's not as if I get invited to weddings all the time," Jono sulked.

"Maybe not to weddings…"

"What else? Being a girl's date at her matric dance or the prom?"

"Why not? Who knows what's around the corner for you? At least, you've met Lerato's boyfriend when you came back. I didn't even know the guy existed until yesterday."

"I thought girls talked about stuff like that."

"She's busy, and I think she wanted to make sure things worked out between the two of them before sharing the news."

"I guess. Lerato has a boyfriend – wow, that puts paid to my chances with her." Jono pulled a funny face and Charlie grinned.

"If you ever had a chance, my boy."

"I guess. How did your murder investigation go?"

"We had a look at the crime scene and the camp where the researchers stayed. There wasn't much in the police report to go on, so inspector Vorster, the homicide detective, drove us to the Kruger without much ado. He's started handling the case here in Joburg before the university got Lerato involved. Not a bad guy but he smiles at me a lot." She shrugged her shoulders.

"And why is that bad?" Jono looked at his sister.

"I just don't like men to look at me that way. Yet. And he's prejudiced when it comes to psychics and me having hunches."

"Oh, that won't work. So Lerato needs you for her new cases as well? I thought you were done with that sort of thing when you came back from Cape Town. Didn't you have an interview with some company lined up?"

"Yeah, but I cancelled. I guess I'm not ready for an 8-to-5-job, and I can hardly say no when Lerato needs my help. Just that I haven't had a single dream about the case. Just a couple of weak hunches. The policeman thought it was funny, but Lerato set him straight."

"And then he stopped smiling at you?"

"He still smiled at me… and the ranger, who was with us, as well."

"Oooh, two guys, who are interested in you! And you didn't dream anything? Now, that's unusual. Do you feel sick or something?"

"Oh stop it. Of course, I still dream, but not about that case. I dreamed about some earrings. We even found earrings just like that, but they turned out not to be relevant to the case. Maybe the dream was symbolic."

"That's something, right? So what else did you dream about?"

"I don't think you want to listen to that!"

"Why not? You always tell me about your dreams, whether I like it or not," Jono laughed. There had been many mornings they'd spent discussing the meaning of Charlie's dreams over breakfast.

"Well okay… I keep having this dream about walking around in some city and the streets are empty. I'm the only person there. Walking across a large square with tall grey buildings all around, and I keep thinking: what the hell happened? Are the people all dead? But then there would be bodies lying around and there are no bodies. Just that the city is completely empty…"

"What? Like the aliens have vaporised everyone in the city or something?"

"Oh come on… aliens!"

"Or people are hiding from a virus the aliens are spreading. Like in 'War of the Worlds' or whatever that movie was called."

"Stop it with the aliens, already."

"Hmmm, do you still have that dream dictionary that explains the meaning of dreams?" Jono wanted to know.

"The one Dad gave me when I was fifteen?"

"Yeah, that one." Jono took a sip of his rooibos

tea. He'd learned long ago not to dismiss Charlie's dreams as nonsense.

"I'm sure I brought it with me. Dad even wrote on the first page. Wait… May only your good dreams come true… but as far as I remember there's nothing in it about walking around a city with nobody in it."

"That's probably too far out. Let's hope you'll go back to normal dreaming soon. Normal for you. It sounds like a complicated case, so it takes a bit longer. I'm sure Lerato appreciates your special skills."

"Special skills. Lol. I always thought that was my training in Genetics. And anyway… you can't rush these things. I keep explaining that to her."

"I've known you long enough to know that, sis. Tell me if I can help you with something." Jono took a bite from his ham sandwich.

"I'll give it some thought. You could start by feeding the dogs. How was your flight to Durban?" Charlie changed the subject and put her cup into the dishwasher. "Want to order in tonight?"

"Sure, we can order Chinese or Sushi. The flight was okay. I flew down with Nico and Frank for the bachelor party. Dave came to fetch us from the airport - the new airport. It's quite a way from Durban, past Verulam. We stayed in a B&B near the Oyster Box Hotel that was supposed to be the venue for the reception…"

"Fancy! A bachelor party, hey?" Charlie winked at her brother.

"NO strippers if that's what you mean," Jono said and put the teacup down.

"Yes, that's what I mean. What did you do, then?"

"We just dressed up in funny clothes. Oversized bow ties and a top hat. Dave was dressed as a bride. He felt so embarrassed. We drove from club to club. Don't worry, it was a taxi-hailing service. We ended up at the Oyster Box. I think I still have a hangover just from that night."

Charlie laughed. "Nobody forced you to drink that much."

"I didn't even have half of what the others had. Can you believe it?"

"Are they closet-alcoholics or what?"

"Probably. Pity that the wedding didn't go ahead. So it was all for nothing."

"At least you had a night out with the boys. Almost a reunion."

"Yeah. I feel sorry for Dave, though. Everything was organised at the hotel then that silly woman has a change of heart. Must have cost an arm and a leg."

"I'm sure Charlene had her reasons."

"Chanelle. There was just too much drama with lots of tears and broken crockery, so I didn't hang around to find out what was going on. Dave has a house down on the coast. All the relatives were staying there. He's making big bucks now with his computer company. Large bedrooms and verandas on two levels. and a swimming pool. His future in-laws stayed in one of the cottages on the property. I don't want to know what was going on there!"

"Sounds like a recipe for disaster. So you fled the scene, so to speak."

"I did. With one of the bridesmaids, who was particularly nice."

"Jono! You didn't make out with her, did you? That's such a cliché. Who was it?"

"Her name's Amy or Ashleigh. I think. Not the blonde one, though. This one has black straight hair. Thin, but quite attractive. "

"You don't remember her name?" Charlie asked.

"Sort of. She's a lab technician in Joburg. That's what I remember because she couldn't shut up about it. The girls came down to Durban in her car for the hen party. Five of them. Two of the bridesmaid's stayed in Durban to console Chanelle, so luckily there was space in the car for me."

"That means somebody will have her number if you want to see her again."

"I haven't had time to think about stuff like that. But she was really pretty."

"We'll have to detox you with rooibos tea for a while, brother dearest. That should clear the brain fog." Charlie shook her finger in Jono's face and he backed away from her, sniggering.

"I don't mind that one bit. I'm off alcohol for a while - and weddings."

Charlie's cell phone rang. 'Oh hi, Lerato. What? Okay. I guess. Yeah, I have something to wear. Speak to you later.'

"Did Lerato make a breakthrough in her case?"

"No, she's still assessing the statements and the evidence. She spoke to some of the suspects again - with the inspector."

"The one that smiles at you?"

"Yes, that one. I'm glad I don't have to be there. I need some time to mull over the whole thing. The statements and the crime scene. Maybe I'll get a real hunch for a change."

"I'm sure you will. So what did she want?"

"There's this formal fundraiser at the university, for the wild dog conservation project. Apparently, that's where I'm going."

"Sounds good. It's time you go out more."

"Yes... by the way, what are you doing Thursday night?"

"Why?'

"Lerato asked me to bring you as my date."

Chapter SEVEN

On Thursday evening, they arrived on campus in time for the event.

"Don't you think I'm a little overdressed?" Jono asked Charlie as he was looking for a spot to park the car close to the hall. Being a jeans and t-shirt kind of guy, he felt uncomfortable in his new suit and tie.

"Oh come on, it's a formal affair. You bought this for your friend's wedding and here's your occasion to wear it. Can't you help your poor old sister out without moaning the whole time?"

"I don't like ties."

"It's not exactly the most comfortable Spandex I'm wearing and high heels are not my favourite shoes, either." Charlie adjusted her bra. "But do you hear ME complaining?"

"Hey, I'm older than you. Show some respect, sis."

"Only by a couple of months," Charlie chuckled. "So there."

Her brother shrugged his shoulders and pulled into

a space on the side of the road, as another car was pulling out. They were supposed to meet Lerato and the inspector at the venue.

Charlie would be talking shop with prospective donors, being a geneticist and all, trying to find out relevant information.

Lerato would make her way to Jeanne Ash-Morton's office in the Botanical Department as soon as an opportunity presented itself. It was a grey legal area, so the inspector had not been let in on it.

"Great, I have to make my way through the ground cover. Alright then, here goes." Charlie hitched up her dress and picked her way through purple grass that edged the kerb, teetering on high heels.

"Well done, sis!" Jono grinned and tucked his arm into hers. "Let's do this thing."

"Thanks, I guess. You look like a regular geek in a suit by the way. I'll probably have to fend off all the women, brother."

"Don't you dare! There must be some benefit in all this for me…"

"As long as you can remember why we are here, you are free to wallow in vice after the event."

"Gee thanks! Wallowing doesn't sound so bad." They both cackled.

Jono would be his sister's date tonight. Officially, she was an associate consultant to the department. Although she had to read up on wild dog projects on Google last night until the wee hours. At least she would be clued up on the subject matter.

Inspector Vorster and Lerato were the other couple with a background story of their own. Guests in formal attire made their way from the parking lot to the venue.

Most of them had paid a small fortune to be here in support of wildlife conservation. Professor Morton's ex-wife was walking ahead of them. She wore a sparkly blue dress and seemed rather absorbed by her conversation with a younger-looking man.

The siblings walked up the stairs to the reception hall. There would be scores of rich and influential people here tonight from all over the world, nibbling on snacks and quaffing champagne.

They would be deciding on a whim, whether they were prepared to throw their wealth at the protection of wild dog in Southern Africa.

A massive banner with a cute wild dog puppy face greeted them at the entrance. "There you are!" Lerato floated towards them in a fabulous cocktail dress that showed off her curves to perfection.

"I thought I would be found out any moment for talking rubbish to these folks. I'm just the girlfriend, but our inspector is doing quite well, I must say!"

"My, my, my - Miss PI, you look simply stunning tonight," Charlie Proudfoot smacked a kiss in the air above Lerato's cheek, trying not to smudge her makeup.

"Right back at you, Miss Associate. And look at you, brother Jono. You should wear suits more often." She winked at him and Jono straightened his back.

"Really? I can't wait to get out of this jacket," he said and offered his arm to his sister again in a gentlemanly gesture.

"And what about me?" Lerato feigned indignation.

"Your date might become jealous, ma'am, eye candy that I am…" Jono laughed.

"Aren't you cute! Our good inspector is over there, somewhere. Ah, there he is."

Lerato pointed to Inspector Marius Vorster. He smiled at them from the other side of the reception area. The elegant women and their smart-looking escort distracted him for a moment from his observation duties.

All he knew was that Charlie Proudfoot would be accompanied by her brother.

"Did you let him in on our little plan?" Charlie whispered to her friend.

"Of course I didn't."

Charlie took two welcoming drinks from a table by the entrance and gave one to Jono. "Don't forget that you're my dedicated driver tonight. So it's juice for now."

"Can't I have a little champagne at least?"

"Okay, but only a little." She poured champagne from a flute into Jono's juice.

"You're so kind," he mocked her.

"Can we move along, please?" A man in a black suit asked impatiently.

"Sorry," Jono said and they stepped aside.

"Careful with that juice, Charlie." Lerato alluded to her friend's insulin resistance.

"I'm not going to drink the juice, but if I'm expected to mingle, I need to hold a glass in my hand. Here we go."

They let the unsmiling man pass and a young student with dreadlocks handed them donation forms. He ticked off their names on the register.

"Thanks!" Jono said and chucked the form under his arm to dispose of it soonest. "Let's see what they have to eat for us. Oh nice, a buffet!"

Lerato nodded and walked towards Marius Vorster. The siblings followed her without protest and ended up in front of the buffet.

"Good evening, Marius."

"You look… beautiful, Ms Proudfoot," the inspector said and Charlie blushed.

"Doesn't she just…" Jono agreed and introduced himself. The two men gave each other mildly suspicious looks, then nodded in a typically masculine fashion. The inspector didn't seem comfortable asking the obvious question: how they could be brother and sister when Jono was clearly Asian. Another time, maybe.

Charlie looked around. Two women in evening suits smiled at her. They were holding champagne glasses in one hand and the donation form in the other. The women carried on chatting as soon as Charlie turned back to her companions.

"Nice to meet you, Jono," the inspector said. "By the way, there will be speeches in about half an hour. All about the research project, according to Dr. Sibanda," the inspector said.

"That won't give us much time to observe and ask questions," Lerato said. "It's best if we grab a plate with a few snacks and then we should circulate. Any news from Sergeant Mokhodi, yet?"

"Yes, he got back to me on the lists I asked him to send."

"That's pretty quick. Anybody on the list we should know?"

"I didn't recognise any of the names, but that doesn't mean much at this stage. I only received it late this afternoon."

"Just forward it to me then I can get Florence to check it out."

"Already done."

"Not bad, thanks. What a drag that Duncey is sticking to his story, almost word for word. But at least the lab is busy with the tyre casts. I'm expecting the results soon. De Vries needed some convincing to foot the bill, but that's just part of my job."

"That's the beauty of working for the State," the inspector said. "It never gets done, but you don't pay for it."

"No thanks, I prefer our version." Lerato inspected the buffet. "Looks good, they even have a rotisserie station."

"Who'll introduce us to the people we need to speak to?" Jono asked and took a plate from the buffet table. "I don't know any of these guests."

He began to heap food onto his plate until he saw Charlie's stern look. Maybe he could do without another prawn…

"Good question. I should think Professor de Vries, but he's all the way over there," Marius Vorster said and got himself a plate. Lerato and Charlie did the same.

"Do you want to get involved in our fact-finding mission?" Charlie asked her brother.

"Why not? Since I'm already here, it doesn't hurt to make myself useful."

"Let me see - Dr. Sibanda is not too far from us. We'll stick with him" Lerato decided. "I'm sure he'll be happy to introduce us to a few people."

Charlie put down her glass and began to eat. "Okay, Prof. de Vries is here, Dr. Sibanda, Prof. Ash-

Morton… who is she speaking to? Posh-looking lady."

"The inspector finished the mini quiche he'd been nibbling on. "I suppose another prospective donor, judging by the way she's dressed."

"I don't see Pericles Duncey or the vet. The student was probably not invited."

"So, they are your suspects?" Jono probed.

"Pretty much."

"Everybody done?" Lerato asked impatiently and put her empty plate on the table. "Come on, people, let's get to work."

"Hey, can't I have seconds?" Jono complained and the women shook their heads.

"No, we are here to speak to people. So let's go. We'll start with Dr. Sibanda."

She steered Charlie and Jono towards the academic and the inspector followed them. "He introduced me to this professor from New York earlier – Prof. Chatelain. Oh, there she is, still talking to him."

Professor Chatelain was probably in her fifties and wore a drop-dead maroon dress with gold trimmings. Her fine, black hair was neatly done up in thin cornrows. It gave her a rebel-like look that was in stark contrast to the sexy outfit.

Lerato walked up to them and jumped right in. "I'm so sorry to interrupt. Good evening, Dr. Sibanda! You remember my associate Ms. Proudfoot? And this is her partner, Mr. Morake. They've just arrived. Marius you've already met."

"Good evening," they greeted each other and nodded.

"Thank you for being here, tonight. May I introduce you? Professor Chatelain lectures Science at the Cooper Union in New York," Dr. Sibanda proudly introduced the woman.

"Oh, isn't Cooper close to Washington Square Park?" Charlie asked.

"It's on Cooper Square. Pleased to meet you," Professor Chatelain's gaze immediately wandered over toward Jono. She seemed to like what she saw.

"Morake is not a very Asian name," the American scientist drawled and virtually ignored Charlie.

"No, you're right, it isn't. I was adopted," Jono said and smiled charmingly. This didn't go unnoticed by the professor from New York and she smiled back at him with a twinkle in her eyes.

"My, my, my. I see that South Africa has changed

quite a lot, since the last time I visited, Tokhozo," she said seemingly taken with Jono.

"Yes, I suppose it has," Dr. Sibanda replied. "Quite a lot."

"And just where did you get that American accent from, darling?" She asked Jono.

"Oh, I grew up in New York, but my adoptive parents are from South Africa."

"Look at that. You're almost a homeboy. Isn't that just amazing? I swear if I was 10 years younger… what area of science do you specialise in?"

"Oh no, I'm not a scientist. I'm in computers, ma'am."

"You don't have to call me ma'am - or do I look that old to you?" The professor seemed a little offended.

"No, not at all," Jono said quickly. He smiled again and Professor Chatelain's expression softened. "Well darling, when you're back in New York, give me a call. We can have coffee," the rather confident woman said. "Or Japanese barbeque." She fished a business card out of her maroon clutch bag.

Jono took the card. "Matilda Chatelain. What a beautiful name. I will most definitely look you up next time I visit my parents in New York. Japanese barbeque sounds good to me."

"Aren't you adorable?" The professor was flattered.

Marius Vorster put his arm around Lerato. "Yes, isn't he just? The two of us on the other hand… need to speak to a friend over there. Good old Jimmy!" He pointed vaguely at the growing crowd. "Please excuse us."

Lerato sneaked a look at her watch. They had lost seven minutes because of Jono's flirting. "Oh yes," she crowed. "Haven't seen Jimmy for a while. It was nice meeting you."

The inspector couldn't help one last charming smile and slight bow before walking off with Lerato. She loosened his grip on her waist. "So much for getting him to introduce us to other guests," she complained.

"Then we'll have to do it ourselves," Marius Vorster said and joined a group of stern-looking men.

Professor Chatelain sighed. "You're so lucky, girl." It was the first time she'd spoken directly to Charlie.

"I guess I am." She beamed at her brother.

Tokhozo Sibanda was one of the suspects, but before Charlie or Jono could ask him any questions, he excused himself. "I'm sorry, I'll be right back. I've just spotted Mrs. Duncey over there. Let me say hello."

"Oh, Mrs. Duncey? Could you point her out to me?" Charlie asked him before he could disappear. Dr. Sibanda pointed to an older lady, who wore a pelt that was hopefully faux fur over an expensive dress. Her hair was done up in a style that was reminiscent of the seventies.

Charlie stretched her neck to get a glimpse of Pericles Duncey's elusive mother, who was now joined by Dr. Sibanda. It was the same woman they had seen talking to the victim's ex-wife earlier. They all seemed to know each other very well.

"So, you said you've been to South Africa before," she addressed the American professor.

"Yes, I'm taking a keen interest in African wildlife and our patrons would like more cooperation with this institute. They do some amazing work. Alas, our university cannot afford to sponsor your programme, but I'm here on behalf of one of our most generous donors."

"I'm glad you came," Charlie said.

"So am I. What did you say you were doing?"

"Oh, I'm an associate consultant for the Department of... Genetics," Charlie answered, taking care to conceal her American accent and the professor's brow smoothed. They briefly discussed the genetics involved in the conservation of wildlife, and Charlie dropped the name of a similar project she had read up on.

"It's a very interesting aspect of conservation. And we are going to run some trials, soon." How easy it was to lie to this woman.

"Is that so?" Professor Chatelain seemed impressed. "You seem to know what you are talking about, young lady. These animals deserve our protection in every possible way."

"Yes indeed, they do." Jono cleared his throat before steering the conversation in a new direction. "I hope the recent murder isn't putting off your patron… and that you'll keep supporting our project."

"Oh, they lend Professor de Vries a helping hand, wherever they can." The feisty American scientist frowned. "What a tragic thing to happen. But the show must go on. Wildlife conservation can't just stop because of this."

The others murmured in agreement.

"Although I'm not sure that William agrees with me."

She pointed to a grumpy-looking gentleman in a

dark suit and red tie, who was standing not far from the bar with two chatty guests. They seemed to grate on his nerves, judging by the look on his face.

"Sorry, William?" Jono asked. "Is he your patron?"

"Well, not the patron I was talking about earlier. This is William Brewster," Prof. Chatelain leaned over with a conspiratorial gesture. "One of THE richest men in America. Oil, of course."

"Oh yes of course," Jono said as if he'd known this all along. "THAT William. Perhaps I should go and talk to the man, see if I can change his mind."

"I'm coming with you, Jono. Nice talking to you, Professor..." Charlie Proudfoot nodded and the scientists nodded back.

"See you later, kids. Enjoy yourselves." She sighed and greeted someone, who'd just arrived.

"So, you'll start trials soon?"

"I don't know, it just slipped out." Charlie felt guilty for making up facts. "William Brewster... he must be Pericles Duncey's cousin."

"Sounds complicated. I'm not even going to try to understand."

Jono picked up two bottles of water from the end

of the bar counter and offered Charlie one of them.

"Thanks, it's getting stuffy in here." She opened the bottle and took a sip. "If Duncey was here, you could call it a clan gathering."

"Alright, let's see what we can get out of Mr. Oil over here."

The noise level had increased as more and more guests were joining the event. The drinks that were served by waiters also contributed to the party aspect.

"… if there is a future in oil or other traditional industries…" The annoying man was in the middle of a dull statement that made Charlie's eyes water.

He had a receding chin and hairline that was as grey as his suit. His wife didn't look much more colourful and stood close behind him. Charlie wondered why this couple were here, they didn't look like donors at all.

Jono stepped up to THE William and bravely interrupted the annoying man's flow of words midsentence.

"Good evening, sir. Jono Morake and this is Ms Proudfoot. Associate consultant. So sorry to interrupt." He gave the couple an apologetic look. "Mr. Brewster, may we have a word with you?"

The grey woman came to life. She snorted and tried to regain the billionaire's attention. "My husband's company is considering…" But it was in vain.

"Excuse me Mrs. –" the oil tycoon said.

"Koekemoer."

"Excuse me Mrs. Koekemoer, but I need to speak to these people. Enjoy the party…"

He looked straight at them before turning his back. The Koekemoers acknowledged defeat. They realised that they'd lost William Brewster's ear – at least for now. Mr. Koekemoer smiled awkwardly and made a beeline for the bar. Another brandy and coke was in order. At least he had the tycoon's business card.

"Bothersome like dog fleas," Mr. Brewster grumbled and addressed Marius. "Can never quite get away from people like that. What can I do for you, sir?"

The big middle-aged man gave him an irritated yet grateful glance. His face was flushed. Where the hell was his valet?

"You are interested in conservation?" Charlie asked the grouchy man. He looked at her briefly, sizing up her breasts before he addressed the young woman.

"A fellow American? Interesting, as long as you

are not one of those insufferable sycophants. The wine is drinkable, but I'm sticking to bottled water from now on." He lifted his water bottle to prove his point and Jono did the same. "Too hot, I say. Too bloody hot in Africa."

Charlie felt like walking away from this arrogant man, but this was business. If this unpleasant man was Duncey's cousin, she needed to get a feel of him. Figuratively speaking. Brewster cracked a smile.

"Compared to this, Texas feels like goddam Sweden." He guffawed and loosened his tie. "Thought it would be easier to deal with the heat," he drawled on. "But it's so unpleasant."

"I see, so you are not particularly fond of wild dogs or Africa..." Charlie stated.

"Ma'am, I abhor both. Dogs are filthy, dirty things... and Africa... well if I'm honest with you, I prefer Hawaii. Much more water there. Normally it's my marketing chief, who discusses new deals, but the man had an accident. Bloody useless, just when I needed him to come to this goddam place. So I decided to take a break and come myself. Bloody mistake if you ask me. Let's get on with it. We still have a few minutes before the presentation starts and I'm damn hungry."

Charlie looked briefly at her watch. "Well, 16 minutes to be exact," she said. "We appreciate your time. Sir, you must have heard of Professor Gerald Morton's sad demise in the Kruger Park a couple of weeks ago. Does that make you less willing to donate to the WDog Project?"

"If that's even possible. Doctor who? Oh yeah, heard of some murder story. Never met the guy. In my eyes, it helps our public image to invest in those projects, murder or not. Just trying to move out of plastics. Very unpopular now. Damn nuisance if you ask me."

"The plastics or the dogs?"

"Both, of course. They are trying to make us clean up the mess in the oceans, but I'm asking you, who benefitted from plastic all those years? The public didn't seem to mind where the stuff was coming from. Damn it all. Some kids make a stink and everything collapses. Now suddenly, it's all my fault…" the man whined.

"What about the wild dogs, then? I understand you are thinking of sponsoring the conservation project."

Charlie didn't bat an eyelash.

"Sure, why not. As I said - for publicity's sake. Dogs are so important – blah blah blah. I have a photoshoot tomorrow and a couple of interviews. One's a press conference, actually. I hate journalists, always digging up dirt then spin that into fake news. But it's important to stay relevant if we want to haul in the big catch."

"What would that big catch be, if I may ask?" Jono and Charlie looked at each other. Were they hitting on something important?

"You may not. Still very hush-hush. Where for the love of God is my valet? That damn clunk was supposed to bring me my food. Bloody useless the lot of them."

"We could go to the buffet," Charlie suggested. "Fancy a bite to eat?"

"Sure, why not?" Jono said. "I'd like to try the prawns."

"Sounds good to me, ma'am." William Brewster glanced at Charlie with a gruff expression. They pushed through the crowd and took plates off the buffet table.

"Hardly anybody knows me here. Feels great for a

change," the billionaire said in a low voice to Jono. "Except for those tedious Cook-Moores. Wonder how they found out, who I am. Ah, at least some real meat. Now that's my kinda food."

He loaded slices of meat onto his plate. A young, muscular man in a suit, obviously his valet, joined them, looking rather nervous. He ducked visibly when Mr. Brewster loaded it over him.

"Where've you been, man? It's your job to protect me from those bloodsuckers. How can you do that if you're nowhere to be seen, I wanna know?"

The valet's eyes were darting to the two guests, who were talking to Mr. Brewster, then he decided that his boss wasn't talking about them.

"My stomach, sir. Suddenly, I just couldn't..."

"Yeah, yeah – stomach," the businessman parroted him without listening. "Do your job, I say. Paying you enough. Your damn luck I won't be firing you. Grab some food, man." The valet obeyed submissively. Of course, he didn't plan on touching the food and making the runs worse, but he dared not gainsay the big man.

Charlie had heard enough from the unpleasant oil

tycoon. There was a big deal in the offing and he was only here for publicity. That could be vital information. She gestured to Jono and they parted ways with Brewster and his valet.

"Wonder what that big catch is, he was talking about," Charlie said. They picked at their food, finally discarding the plates on the counter.

"I'm sure Lerato will get onto it."

"Yeah, she will. Bah, I think I need a shower." Charlie shook herself. "Is there any cliché that guy didn't tick? There is something about him. I mean he doesn't give a hoot about wildlife and just thinks about himself."

"At least he was grateful that we saved him from the 'dog fleas'. And he's here for something else."

The big catch..." A screeching noise startled Charlie. "Ouch!"

Someone was testing the microphone at the far end of the room where the presentation was being prepared. Lerato was nowhere to be seen.

They heard Mr. Brewster guffaw in an oily sort of way and briefly looked back at the two men. William Brewster was apparently in a much better mood, tucking into his roast beef. His valet stood there with hunched shoulders, scrunching up his face as he chugged back the dark liquid in a shot glass. He put the shot glass next to a Jägermeister bottle on the bar counter and William Brewster clapped the man's shoulder, laughing.

"Odd man. Wonder if all that money gets to people after a while… what's that guy's name? The billionaire, who now lives in Canada?"

"Canada? Elon Musk?" Charlie suggested.

"Yes, that guy. Also too rich for his own good. Used to be a nice South African bloke…"

They walked past well-dressed academia and arrogant-looking suits. Some of the guests were already facing the big white screen in the corner where Professor de Vries would give his speech in less than 5 minutes. The microphone gave off another loud screech.

"Dammit!" Charlie swore and held her hands to her ears. "I hate that noise."

"Let's find a good spot," Jono suggested.

The jazz tunes that had been playing in the background died down. A student fiddled with a laptop on the table next to the white screen and a

PowerPoint presentation popped up on the screen behind her.

"Excuse me please… I'll be right back," Lerato said to the businessmen she had been chatting to. She passed the siblings and gave them the thumbs up.

"Keep an eye on Prof. Ash-Morton. I'm going in," Lerato whispered in Jono's ear.

He nodded and she was gone. The PI made her way to the Botany section as they had discussed. A man next to them held his champagne glass at an odd angle and Jono saved him from embarrassment with a quick move.

"Oops. Thank you. Sorry, lady…" he apologised to a woman behind him.

"Bad thing about the murder of Professor Morton, hey?" Jono said. "Somebody told me about it only a couple of days ago."

"A small blip on the crime radar in South Africa," he said.

"Oh really?"

Jono was surprised at the callous response.

"It won't keep us from doing business or South Africa will fall into ruin."

Jono smiled drily at him. He bit back the sarcastic remark that was sitting on the tip of his tongue. Then the room went dark and all conversations died down. As soon as the lights were dimmed, everybody's attention turned to Prof. de Vries and the images on the screen behind him.

"Thank you so much, everybody, for attending this donor-event. My name is Professor de Vries from the Department of Zoology. I'm standing in for Professor Gerald Morton and I hope you will forgive me the occasional gremlin that might slip in," the Dean began his speech. "On behalf of the university, I would like to welcome everybody, who has travelled here from far and wide and your interest in our conservation efforts. A special welcome also to the deputy minister of the Department of Environment, Forestry and Fisheries. Thank you for being here."

There was some feeble clapping and somebody drew his attention to a typing error in the title of the first slide.

"May the person, who invented autocorrect, burn in hello," Prof. de Vries joked and the illustrious audience erupted in laughter.

*

Lerato heard the laughter as she crept along the hallways that looked more or less all the same to her at every turn. It had been a good idea to study the layout and she was pretty sure that this was the right way.

Once again, she turned away from security cameras on her route. A student with acne greeted her politely on the stairs.

"Good evening Dr. Mazibuko." He kept marching in the opposite direction. Good lord, somebody thinks I'm a Dr. Mazibuko, she thought. That might come in handy at some point. Dr. Mazibuko – that had a ring to it.

She smiled and kept on walking confidently down the passage as her heels made a clacking noise on the polished floor. It didn't take her long to find the door to the professor's office upstairs. The doors on either side of the passage were near identical. Except for the name on the brass plaque:

Botanical Sciences

Prof. Jeanne Ash-Morton

Lecturer

Opening the door was child's play. Andy Malherbe, Lerato's partner at the agency, had taught her the tricks of the trade. I have to show Charlie how to do that, she thought fleetingly and turned the doorknob. The office of Prof. Morton's ex-wife was dark, but Lerato didn't touch the light switch. A faint shaft of light fell through a narrow glass window above the door and onto the linoleum floor.

After closing the heavy door as silently as possible, she used her cell phone's torchlight to search the large desk closer to the back wall. If Pericles Duncey was to be believed, she would find some key evidence right there in this desk. So here goes, she thought and probed the top.

It was almost too orderly for such a busy professor. Even the IN and OUT baskets were neat and tidy and contained only a few memos. She opened the top drawer. It yielded nothing but pens and markers and a spare car key to the left and lecture notes to the right. A small whiskey flask was tucked underneath the notes.

Had Pericles Duncey made the whole story up to distract attention away from him? It was certainly a possibility.

Lerato began to wonder if this search wasn't a total waste of time when she tried to open the bottom drawer. It didn't budge and she took the little appliance that had already helped her open the door lock. She pushed the dustbin out of the way a little too vehemently and the bin fell over with a metallic clank.

The PI stopped in her tracks and remained immobile for a good minute or so. Everything stayed quiet. She took a deep breath and picked up some of the crumpled papers that lay on the floor.

What do we have here? She shone her torchlight on a receipt for some medication and what looked like a personal note, but there was no time to study the contents.

Lerato put the receipt and the note into her evening bag before tossing crumpled papers and a brown apple core back into the bin. Yuck.

She wiped her fingers on her evening jacket and moved the bin carefully to the side before opening the drawer without much effort.

Lerato realised within seconds that she had struck gold this time. She photographed the contents of the folder with her cell phone. There were 17 pages in all. Working fast, she turned the pages in the same order as she had found them.

She studied the last page and was concentrating so

hard that she almost missed a faint creaking sound. Lerato looked up.

There was that creaking sound again! Had she forgotten to lock the door? She stood stock-still and watched the doorknob move.

Chapter EIGHT

What to do? Her mind raced. The last page had a bunch of signatures on it that might prove important. Should she switch the torchlight off and hide? But where? The doorknob clicked.

The private detective coolly turned her attention back to the last page and took a picture. Then she took her gun out and positioned herself behind the door, trying to calm her breathing. Damn, the drawer was still open and the folder on the desktop… and the bin was visible from the door. The door rattled and the hinges rasped.

Lerato had no choice but to wait. She held her weapon above her head and kept watching the door. The lock jammed with a dull thump and Lerato dared to breathe again. She lowered her gun and holstered it, then relaxed her muscles. *I didn't forget to lock the door after all!*

Unless this person had a key for the door, which was still a possibility, she had a minute to think. Now it was a question of getting out of this stuffy, windowless room. A plan… she needed a plan!

First, the bin needs to be moved back in place, then… She tensed up when she heard a soft rap on the wooden door.

"Lerato… are you in there?" A familiar male voice whispered outside and her relief was intense. It was Jono!

Lerato opened the door and Jono slid through the crack into the dark room. "Everything alright, here?"

"It was - before you turned the doorknob," she hissed. "Just stay where you are. I'm about to wrap things up!" Lerato got to work quickly with just enough light coming in through the glass panel above the door.

Jono watched her place the document she had so painstakingly photographed back where it belonged. Then she locked the drawer and gave the office a last once-over. Everything needed to look exactly the way it had when she'd entered the room.

The dustbin was the last detail and she moved it back to where she'd found it. Lerato made sure she had her gun and her cell phone before turning her attention to Jono.

"Why did you follow me? You nearly gave me a heart attack!" She scolded him.

"Sorry about that. They started the Q & A part and I thought you might want to know," Jono said and took a step toward the door. They still whispered.

"Yes, yes sure, thanks. Let's get out of here before de Vries is finished."

"Did you find anything?"

"I think so." Lerato opened the door a crack and peeked out. "The coast is clear. Let's get going!"

They encountered only two students in the dimly-lit passage as they made their way downstairs. Again, Lerato was greeted as Prof. Mazibuko.

"Professor Mazibuko?" Jono chuckled.

"Don't ask. I seem to have a Doppelgänger."

A few guests were chatting outside the open doorway. One of the men was decidedly drunk and had taken his seat on the floor, holding his head in his hands. Jono and Lerato looked at each other and rolled their eyes.

There was a space in front of the buffet.

"...of course that's not all." Deon de Vries sounded like a snake oil salesman. "To show our appreciation for your generosity, we would like to invite you on a brief tour to see the wild dogs in the Kruger Park. Date of the trip is the 27th. The day after tomorrow. We'll stay over in one of the camps for just one night then travel back to Johannesburg by plane on the 28th. The top ten most generous donors are guaranteed a seat." He held up the donor form. "You may give your form to this young lady here." De Vries pointed to the student, who had been operating the laptop. "Any more questions?"

On the screen, enticing images of a campsite with laughing tourists took turns with scenes of wild dogs that carried pups and a leopard in a tree. Gerald Morton must have taken those pictures on the last day of his life.

There was a shocked murmur in the audience when the leopard appeared.

"Is the pack taking the puppies away because of the leopard?"

"Yes, we do believe that Pack D3 moved dens because of this magnificent cat." Professor de Vries explained. The cute image of playing pups popped up on the screen and didn't fail to make an impression.

"Aaawww."

The professor let the image sink in for a few moments. "Our magician will start his programme in a little while. I'm told that he's stuck in traffic. If there are no more questions… please enjoy the rest of your evening."

The WDOG logo replaced the picture of the wild dog puppies and the room burst into applause. The lights came on and the smooth jazz tunes resumed. The bar was swamped, and a line of hungry guests was forming in front of the buffet.

A young woman in a waiter's uniform was clearing away abandoned glasses and plates while another one topped up the near-empty biltong bowls.

"There you are." Charlie and the inspector leisurely joined them at the buffet. "All good?" Charlie whispered in Lerato's ear.

"More than good."

"I wonder what de Vries was so worried about. These people don't seem to care much about the murder case," Inspector Vorster said.

"Could we get something to eat?" Jono mewled. "I'm starving."

"You're insatiable," Charlie grinned at her brother.

"Let's hurry then before the food's all gone."

"Now there's a good idea," Marius Vorster said. "The speech made me hungry. How long is this event?"

"I'd say the formal part is as good as over. Just the entertainment bit."

"Then we should speak to a few more people."

"Damn all the prawns are gone…" Jono complained.

"But there are still plenty of sausage rolls."

Plates in hand, they chatted to a British journalist, who was helping himself to some sausage rolls. He told them with an important air that he would also be at the press conference the following day.

"It's not a very interesting subject for our viewers, but we'll do our best to draw more attention to the plight of endangered wildlife. And someone like William Brewster, tosser as he might be, will definitely draw attention to the cause." The journalist took a sip from his champagne glass. "Wonder what happened to Pericles Duncey. He was supposed to be here tonight."

"Yes, I was also wondering," Lerato said. "Haven't seen him all night."

"He was touted THE South African investor - he and his mother Elise. Very wealthy family. Most of the money's inherited."

"From John Brewster, if I'm not mistaken," Lerato said matter-of-factly. This journalist was turning out to be a goldmine of information.

"Also a cousin of William Brewster."

"So it's all in the family?"

"So to speak. I'm surprised that the man himself is here tonight. All the way from the States. Usually, he just sends one of his minions," the journalist said. "I wanted to ask Duncey a few questions about that top-secret new project he's got going with Brewster and a few other investors. Top-secret my ass. My contact at the patent office keeps me updated."

"Oh, that's interesting."

"Perhaps Duncey's around here somewhere," Charlie played the issue down. "He wouldn't miss a glamourous event like this one. Doesn't the new project involve a plant remedy?"

"I'm pretty sure, he isn't here. Duncey, I mean," the tipsy journalist insisted. "And yes, they're testing some virus-busting plant extract. Rumour has it that the two Mortons didn't agree on some issue. Now there might be a headline in it. Maybe I should ask you a few questions instead…"

"Oh, I don't think so. I could only regurgitate a few rumours I've heard. You'd better stick with Mr. Duncey or Mr. Brewster."

"What did you say you were doing at the department?"

"Oh, I'm just an associate. Genetics. Nothing too exciting."

The audience began to clap. The magician had arrived and began his programme. He was right on the money, as the guests were enthralled by his inventive tricks.

Jono traded witty repartees regarding current American politics with the journalist and tried to find out what he knew about the murder case. To his disappointment, it turned out that the journalist didn't know anything new.

This event was dragging on and the ladies here were out of his league. "Oh hello."

"Hello, nice of you to join us," Jono greeted Professor Chatelain with a charming smile. At least the American scientist was more entertaining. She approached with two women in tow and introduced them.

"Pleased to meet you," Jono said and kissed each woman's hand.

"How gallant," the American gushed and winked playfully at Jono. "Don't you just love the magician?"

"Yes, very entertaining," he agreed.

"Did you know Professor Morton?" Marius Vorster asked. Why waste time?

"I met the poor man a year ago in London," the woman from Malaysia said. Her head was wrapped in a colourful silk scarf. "Shocking. Such a bright mind and very passionate about wild animals."

"Not the only thing he was passionate about." The woman from France spoke in a deep, heavily accented voice. Her dress was very fashionable and her lipstick mirrored the same shade of pink.

"Oh, how so?" The inspector asked her.

"Well, you know… he had an eye for the ladies," the French woman said in a loud whisper. "No surprise with a wife like that. Enough said." She giggled like a teenager.

"That's a long time ago, Marielle," Professor Chatelain corrected her. "He hasn't had an affair in *years*."

"Unfortunately," the French woman moaned in jest and winked at Charlie.

"I didn't know him well," Charlie said in a distracted tone and looked past her at a man in khaki shirt and trousers.

The French woman turned her attention back to Marius Vorster. Meanwhile, Charlie stared at the khaki-clad man. He was out of place in a room full of formally dressed people, but nobody seemed to mind him. His face was pale and his blue eyes didn't have a shine to them. She felt inexplicably drawn to this strange man, who beckoned with his pale hand.

Charlie looked around and realised that he meant her.

She had seen this face before! But where? No, she thought, that can't be.

"Excuse me please." Charlie made her way through the crowd towards the man. Before she reached him, however, he turned around to walk ahead of her and she saw a dark mass below the rim of his sunhat. Dried blood.

She simply had to follow him and that's what she did.

Everyone watched the talented magician, how he threw a packet of cards in the air, then caught the one a volunteer from the audience had chosen. Applause.

"Aren't you Professor Morton? Where are we going?" She cried a trifle high-pitched amidst the clapping.

Nobody but her could see the spectre, and a couple of guests closest to her turned around to stare. A man in a snazzy suit sniggered and made a drinking gesture to his companion. She gave him a stern look and walked past the men.

Charlie was everything but drunk. Quite the opposite. This sudden turn of events felt somehow exhilarating. Finally, she was making progress!

They reached the door and the ghostly man led the way past the drunk, who was still sitting on the floor, and down the dimly-lit passage ahead of Charlie. She vaguely remembered that the Zoological Faculty was on the same floor as the venue room.

So this... whatever it was... was heading straight for the Zoology Department, where Professor Morton had worked.

They passed greeting students, who were oblivious to the man guiding her.

"Good evening ma'am."

"Good evening," she answered with a smile, trying not to lose the man in khaki around the next corner.

The spectre took a left turn around a wooden filing cabinet that had seen better days. Charlie briefly looked at pictures of a caterpillar, a chrysalis and a butterfly on the opposite wall and kept following him.

Morton suddenly stopped in front of another picture that showed the lungs of a green arboreal snake. He beckoned, his bluish lips forming the word 'come', then slid through a massive wooden door. He'd moved right through the door!

"Wait, where did you go? I can't follow you through a door. Talk to me!"

But the man had disappeared into the room and there was no answer. She stepped forward to read the sign on the door:

Zoological Sciences

Professor Dr. Gerald Morton

Head of Department

Charlie jiggled the doorknob, but it didn't budge.

Locked, of course! Perhaps he would reappear and she'd find out what this was all about. She took a step back and waited in front of the snake picture, but the man apparition remained elusive. When she heard echoing steps approaching from the other side of the passage, she started walking back the way they had come.

What are you trying to tell me? She thought forcefully. A young man rushed past with a wad of papers in his hand. Gee, people are working late around here. It was easy to get lost in these passages and Charlie followed the young guy's echoing steps down the passage and towards the stairs.

Meeting the spectre had left her in a strange mood. Why was she able to see, and even communicate to an extent, with a deceased stranger, but not her own husband, who had perished in a tragic car accident?

Why couldn't she just will him to come to her? Oh, how she longed to see him one more time and ask Colin what had happened that night, if he was with their unborn child and whether he knew anything about that accident that she didn't know… She reigned her thoughts in. This was not the time or place.

She took a deep breath and hurried on. Lerato was probably wondering where she had disappeared to. She was distracted and barely noticed Irina Lotcombe walking past with a smile.

When she returned, Jono, Lerato and the inspector stood in front of the bar. The three women had gone mingling with other guests.

"Where have you been?" Her brother asked. "You just walked away and we were getting worried."

"Can I have some water?" Charlie asked.

"Water?" The inspector asked.

"Why not?" Jono gave her the bottle he was holding.

"Thank you. Can I speak to you?" She asked Lerato.

Marius Vorster studied her face. Was he trying to use x-ray vision on her?

"Sure, what's up?" Lerato answered.

"It's a women's thing."

"What women's thing?" Lerato shot back, but quickly realised that it was code for *I need to speak to you alone*. "Okay, we can talk over there. Be right back, guys."

The men looked a little confused. None of them wanted to know what women's thing Charlie was talking about.

"We'll stay here and grow roots, then," Jono said a little miffed. He couldn't wait to get out of the suit.

"You can have the last of the samosas!" Lerato

said and they all laughed. She pulled Charlie by the elbow to one of the large windows. Out of earshot.

"Okay spill," Lerato demanded. "What's so important that you can't say it in front of the others'?"

"I'm not sure how to tell you this…" Charlie spoke in hushed tones.

"You're pregnant?"

"What? No, of course not. Why would I be pregnant?" Charlie snapped.

"Okay, you're not… so what's up?"

"I saw him... I saw the murder victim here in the room! He was wearing khaki clothes and a hat, and he was standing right there in the audience, waving for me to follow him. It was so weird…"

Lerato stared at her. She didn't quite know what to say. "And you went with him?"

Her eyes grew bigger, as Charlie continued. "Yes, of course, I did. He was so pale and there was dried blood on the nape of his neck - just below the rim of his hat. And he looked just like he did in the crime scene photos. We went down the passage and ended up in front of his office. Then he disappeared through the door. Through the closed door!"

"So it was just like the thing you saw in Port Elizabeth?"

A man lifted his champagne glass and smiled at Charlie. She tried to ignore him. "Not exactly the same thing. It was more like a real…"

"I knew it. It's not just intuition with you!" Lerato raised her voice.

"Ssshhh, keep it down. Maybe… but that's not important now. Did you hear what I said? He disappeared into his office. He mouthed 'come' and then went through the door, somehow. The door was locked, so I couldn't get in."

"Maybe I searched the wrong office tonight."

"What do you mean? I thought you already found something important."

"Yes, I did. But there must be another reason why he took you all the way up to his office. Something must be in there that can help us solve the case. Oh, I'm getting goosebumps all over just thinking about it."

"It felt a bit spooky, especially when he disappeared through that door."

"Wow, first nothing and now this! I hired you for your intuition, doll, but I never expected anything like this!"

"I wonder what's in that office."

"Maybe the police missed something during their search or they didn't know what they were looking at. Or maybe this professor-woman hid something and the ghost wanted to show it to you. There are so many possibilities. I'll speak to Marius and…"

"And tell him what? You have to come up with some explanation, why you want to search the office."

"Then I'll come up with something. You okay?"

Charlie's face looked a little pinched. "I don't know – I'm still a little rattled." She took a swig from the water bottle. "That's never happened to me before."

Jono touched Charlie's shoulder from behind. "Hey sis, not done talking yet?"

"Gee, Jono, want me to jump out of my skin?! Don't do that!" Charlie took a deep breath and glared at her brother.

"Sorry. Didn't mean to frighten you," Jono apologised. "We're just tired of waiting."

"Yeah well. Don't sneak up on me like that!" She snapped at him

"Gee, I won't. Can we go now, please? I'm tired of this crowd and all this talk about oil fields in Iraq and the gold price and denning wild dogs."

"We were just finished talking, so you're in luck. I'll give you a call in the morning," Lerato said to Charlie. "Go home and have a rest. We'll go over the document I found you-know-where first thing. Then we'll take it from there. You can leave that plate with me."

Jono handed her the plate he was holding and Lerato nibbled on one of the samosas while she walked back to speak to the inspector.

"What will you figure out tomorrow?" Jono asked his sister on the way to the parking lot. As was to be expected, some of the guests had too much to drink and cars from a taxi-hailing service were lined up outside.

"I didn't want to tell you guys in front of the inspector, but I saw a ghost earlier. I followed a fricking ghost, Jono. Professor Morton, the murder victim…"

She told him what she had told Lerato.

"Wow, far-out! The murder victim is now appearing to you? And here I thought the document Lerato found was the firecracker. Are you sure, your Dad wasn't an Irishman?" He unlocked the car.

"Pretty sure. Gosh, these heels are killing me!"

She tossed her shoes on the back seat. "Can you drive, please?"

"Sure. I was drinking juice and water most of the time. Good to know that we didn't waste all this precious time and no results. Marius was a bit frustrated until we spoke to the journalist. So what happens now? Does this help you with the case?"

"I guess. We'll probably have to involve the police... to search Morton's office again because that's where the spectre took me."

"You want Marius to search the office without telling him about the ghost? You'll have to spin quite a story."

"I'll leave that up to Lerato. She's an experienced ex-policewoman and I'm sure she's talking to him right now." Charlie put her hand over her eyes.

"Hey sis, you seem a bit nervy."

"Yeah, I have to get my head around this... ghost. What I saw in Port Elizabeth was nowhere near as intense. And then, we spoke to all these people..."

"Maybe, if you let it sink in, something crops up?" Jono suggested.

"Yes, that's possible. Did you go to the ex-wife's

office with Lerato?"

"I did and I'm sure, Lerato will tell you all about that document she found."

"She'll tell me in the morning. There was just no time to discuss it. That damn ghost should have said something then I'd know more."

"Maybe he can't speak..." Jono shook himself. "Phew! Imagine a speaking ghost. As long as he doesn't follow us home..."

"Nah, he won't," Charlie assured him. "But you know who I wish would follow us home?"

"Who?" Her brother asked suspiciously as he followed other cars to the boomed exit. The security guard gestured for the driver in front of them to press a large red button and Jono rolled down his window.

"I wish that I could see Colin and speak to him about everything that's happened. It's been tough since he... left."

"I know, sis, but you never know. One day, maybe."

Jono steered the car while Charlie leaned back and closed her eyes. He pressed the large red button and waved to the guard. The boom opened and they drove off the university grounds.

Chapter NINE

The policewoman tried to sound firm. "I understand, ma'am, but we have a search warrant for your husband's office. Will you please step aside?"

The woman in the expensive black & white dress stood her ground.

"Ex-husband - and no, I can't let you do this! It's outrageous!" Professor Ash-Morton was beginning to lose her cool. To her mind, she had valid reason to worry. "We have important papers and specimens stored in there – after your colleagues rummaged through everything. If you mess it all up, it will take forever to…"

They argued in front of the office next to a framed picture of a green Australian tree snake.

"Madam, you are interfering with a murder investigation. You saw the search warrant and the inspector will be here any minute. Don't make me arrest you, please." The policewoman said coolly. She was a little in awe of the smartly dressed professor and her arrogance irked her at the same time.

"You would arrest me for trying to preserve important paperwork?" The professor asked in a waspish tone.

"Only if I have to - madam."

By the time the Head of Department arrived, a group of wide-eyed students and university staff had assembled outside the office door pushing up against each other. The picture of the green tree snake came crashing down next to the policewoman and everybody jumped.

"I didn't touch it. You saw me not touching it, right?" Jeanne Ash-Morton addressed the audience. Some looked embarrassed. What was going on, here?

"Thank God, there you are, Deon," she said relieved. "They want to search Gerald's office again. Can you imagine the mess they will be making?"

"I don't see that we have much of a choice." Professor de Vries was clearly on the side of the policewoman. That could get interesting.

"But they've already seen the office, the last time the police were here."

"Be reasonable, Jeanne," Prof. de Vries said to

calm her down. "I like it as little as you do, but we must cooperate with the police in this."

"Must we now?" The woman flared up. A man in a dark suit arrived, flashing an ID card in front of her nose. "Yes," Inspector Phaladi confirmed. "You must. Sergeant…"

He gave the policewoman a brief nod.

Jeanne Ash-Morton's face crumpled. She exhaled angrily and moved aside. Her high heels crunching on the broken glass. "Very well," she mumbled with a piqued expression.

"Thank you, madam." Inspector Phaladi stepped forward and unlocked the office door. The audience held their breath and – were not disappointed.

The door swung back with a creaking sound, revealing a large stain on the office floor! It looked a lot like congealed blood and the inspector narrowly managed to avoid stepping into it. Everybody stared in delicious shock.

"What on earth is that?" Jeanne Ash-Morton stepped back and grew rather pale.

The policewoman, who was standing next to her, recovered before anyone else did. It was not the first pool of blood she had seen in her two years in Homicide and this one was no different than any other case. They had to investigate the likelihood of a dead body in this office. She joined inspector Phaladi in the office, side-stepping the bloodstain.

"We need to cordon off the scene, Khumalo," the inspector addressed a policeman in charge of keeping the spectators at bay. "Get CSI to come out."

Officer Khumalo got onto his phone immediately and another policeman took over from him. "Keep moving, please. Let us do our job. thank you… keep moving."

Of course, nobody wanted to keep moving. This was too good to be true. Cell phones came out and selfies were taken with the bloodstain in the background.

"Is this the reason why you wouldn't open the door, Jeanne?" Deon de Vries asked softly. "What on earth happened here?"

The botanist stood frozen in the doorframe and stared at the stain. The implications of this discovery began to dawn on her. "I swear I have nothing to do with that." She pointed to the stain.

The policewoman reappeared and shook her head at the inspector. She had checked behind piles of boxes with papers and books and there was no dead body to be found. The inspector was visibly relieved, although there was still the mystery of the bloodstain to solve.

"Do you have any explanation for this?" He asked Jeanne Ash-Morton.

"I… I was just worried about his research, that it might become a mess before we can sort through everything. But this blood… I have no idea how this could have possibly gotten here... I have no explanation…" she stuttered.

Her answer was not good enough for the police inspector. "Who else has the key to this office?"

"Currently, just me…"

"That leaves me no choice. Jeanne Ash-Morton, we are taking you downtown for questioning…" Inspector Phaladi said firmly. "You are the boss here?" He addressed Professor de Vries.

"Yes…yes, I'm the Dean of the faculty," Professor de Vries said.

"Can you show Sergeant Motlabi and Prof. Ash-Morton to a quiet room, please?"

"Well yes, follow me."

"I swear, Deon, I have no idea what this is all about." Jeanne Ash-Morton said to the Dean as she followed him with the female sergeant.

He held up his hand in a defensive gesture. "Spare me, Jeanne… who would have thought you were capable of something like this?"

"But it wasn't me…" The woman insisted feebly.

"Keep the crime scene secured, Sepele," the inspector said to one of the police constables. "Khumalo, did you get hold of CSI?"

"Yes, sir! Williams is at another crime scene, but I tried Ramogatse. Her line's still engaged." The police officer reported.

"Keep trying. The sooner they can get here, the sooner we'll be out of here."

Khumalo was already on his phone, speaking to one of the crime investigators on duty. "Ramogatse says she'll be here in 20 minutes, sir."

"20 minutes? Better than nothing. I'll go with the suspect and question her here so long. We can take her down to the station later. You stay here and keep an eye on things with Sepele. Telephonic feedback in half an hour."

"Yes, sir!" Khumalo said and held his hand out when a small group of female students tried to push up against the crime scene tape. "You can't get through here. This is a crime scene. Take another route."

The young women, who were used to getting their way, gave him a mouthful, but the sergeant remained stern. "You are here to learn, but you can't even listen? Wena, go the other way!"

Eventually, the students complied, but not without glancing inside the open office.

Needless to say that the bloodstain went viral on social media that day and rumours started flying all over campus.

*

"How did you get them to search the office again?" Charlie asked her friend after they'd registered at the front desk.

"Easy. Only that we didn't get a chance to see it."

Charlie Proudfoot and Lerato Gwala had just arrived downtown at the police headquarters and entered interrogation room no. 5. Inspector Vorster was outside to take an important phone call and nodded in greeting.

They sat down opposite the suspect and waited for the inspector to come back inside.

"Excuse me. May I have a look at the soles of your shoes?" Charlie asked Professor Ash-Morton on the spur of the moment.

"And why would you want to do that?" The woman snapped. She had crossed her arms and was not in the best of moods.

"I need to establish a fact…"

"Very well!" Reluctantly, the suspect lifted her fancy Louboutin shoes with a sullen look on her face. First one then the other. She showed Charlie the soles, then moved her feet under the table as if to hide them.

"Happy?" She asked in a snarky tone.

"Very. Thank you."

Inspector Vorster walked in with cups of coffee, but the professor pushed her cup away from her with an air of disdain. "I'm sure it tastes like dishwater."

"Can't fault her on that one," Lerato said.

"Do you have still water?" The woman demanded.

"Only tap water, madam," the sergeant by the door said.

"Never mind then…"

"Could you lift your feet again? Or better yet, take the shoes off for us to inspect?" Charlie asked her.

"Whatever for?" Jeanne Ash-Morton rolled her eyes, but complied and took her shoes off handing them to Charlie. The sooner they were done with this, the sooner she could get back to work.

"The soles of these pumps are red, but I cannot detect any blood on them," Charlie said. "Also, the toe is pointed and the imprint on the floor has a round toe. Inspector Vorster took a look and nodded.

His colleague, inspector Phaladi, had been called to another homicide and handed the suspect over to him an hour ago. Right from the word go, she had insisted that she knew nothing about the blood on the office floor.

"Could we have a word with you outside, please?" Lerato picked up her coffee and pointed to the passage outside.

"How long are you going to keep me here?" The suspect called after them and the police officer guarding her stood upright. "I wish to speak to my attorney now!"

"Sit down please, madam," the policewoman

ordered her.

The detective went to the coffee nook down the hall. "Darn, now she's asking for an attorney. I really have to make it stick otherwise we'll have to release her asap." Inspector Vorster grabbed a chair and put his cup on the table.

"She wasn't there," Lerato said. "Those are the same shoes she wore last night. Plus there's no body anywhere near that office. No drag marks either."

"The footprints lead to boxes to the left and then out the door," Charlie added. "There are a couple of very faint prints in the passage. Thankfully the floor hasn't been cleaned. No offence."

"None taken. It's not my university after all." the inspector grinned.

"The footprints were made by a woman's shoe," Lerato summarised. "Just not by her." She took a sip of her coffee and put the cup on the counter. "Not one speck of blood."

"How do you know the blood got there last night?" The inspector asked.

"Because, according to Prof. de Vries, the last boxes were moved from Dr. Sibanda's office just before the fundraiser last night."

"To double-check, you can always test the shoes with that spray you guys use," Charlie said. Lerato nodded. "Luminol. And, the body wasn't lifted up magically and beamed out of there."

"So where did the blood come from?"

"I wouldn't be surprised if it's a prank," Charlie said.

"A prank?"

"Yes, what else makes sense?"

"CSI are testing the blood, just in case. We'll have to let her go. I'll keep you in the loop if we find something."

"Thanks. We'll be on our way, then."

The inspector stood up and walked Lerato and Charlie to the glass door.

"It would be great if we could have the results by tomorrow, Marius."

"I'll see what I can do to speed things up."

"It's only blood," Lerato rolled her eyes. "Just send me the notes and your recording as a voice note, so we have something to work with."

"Yes ma'am," the inspector opened the glass door for them and went back into the interrogation room to tell Jeanne Ash-Morton that she was free to go.

*

"Great sleuthing, partner," Lerato whistled through her teeth as they walked down the stairs into the parking garage. The lift was out of order. "I didn't know she was wearing the same shoes last night. Well observed. We'll make a proper detective out of you yet."

"Oh no, I've no desire to become a proper detective. Just helping you out with this case. I'm still sifting through everything that happened yesterday at the fundraiser. For instance, why the ranger and de Vries were going on about our murder victim being a stud with women, and that jealousy could be a motive. But Professor Chatelain didn't seem to agree with that. So something doesn't gel here. What do you think?"

"Hmm, not sure. If anyone seems to know about things like that, it's her. The way she came onto Jono." Lerato smacked a kiss in the air.

"Yes, my brother seemed to enjoy the attention, too… then Gerald Morton just pops up in the middle of everything and takes me to his office… and voilà: there's blood on the floor. How does that fit together with the murder?"

"That must have been something. Weird how he didn't speak to you."

"My hair is still standing on end when I think about it." Charlie shook herself.

"Not to mention my little excursion to our new suspect's office. I'm just glad it all went well. Somehow it doesn't feel right that Marius Vorster's the only one not in the loop. He seems to be a decent policeman."

"Yeah... as long as it takes us somewhere. Do you want to tell me about the document you found last night?"

"Sure... where did I park the car?" Lerato searched in her bag for the keys.

"Visitor parking, remember?"

"We can go to the campus for a bite to eat. I could use real coffee. Then we..."

Lerato couldn't finish her sentence. A shot exploded in the confined space of the parking garage and echoed between the concrete walls. A bullet whistled past Lerato's head. There was no doubt about it: this shot had been aimed at Lerato!

The two women ducked behind the concrete staircase. Following her police-instinct, the PI took out her gun. She held it straight up against the side of her head and motioned for her friend to stay down, then peeked around the narrow wall in front of the staircase.

"Gamoto!" Charlie whispered. "You're bleeding…"

Lerato squatted next to her. She touched her temple and saw the blood. "Just a scratch. Where's security? Masende exwhele!" The Xhosa expression had slipped out against her better judgment, but she could be sure that Charlie didn't understand the expletive.

"No point in calling the police. We are at the police headquarters!" Charlie hissed. She took out a wad of tissues and handed it to Lerato.

The parking garage came to life. There was shouting and running.

"Bloody hell!" A flustered Charlie pointed to the stairs. "Go back?"

Lerato shook her head. "Wait!" She whispered. The shouting was getting louder as armed security personnel moved in. Somebody was ordered to lie flat on the ground, hands behind his neck.

"Finally!" Lerato helped Charlie up. "I think it's safe now. They got them!"

Lerato put her gun back into the holster and they

walked towards a crowd by the entrance.

A man in a dark t-shirt and jeans was lying on the ground, facing the hard concrete. His hands were bound with cable ties on his back. One security guard was enraged that the tsotsi had tried to get past his watchful eye. He had his boot firmly on the neck of the shooter and nobody objected. Another guard went to shut down a blaring car alarm. Charlie saw Marius Vorster come toward them.

"Everything alright?" He gave Lerato a worried glance. "You better get that looked at." He yelled to someone to bring bandages.

"There's only one shooter?" Charlie asked the inspector and noticed that her hands trembled. "It sounded like a small army."

"As far as I can tell."

"This bhentse emfene was shooting at us over there." Lerato turned around and pointed to the concrete wall in front of the staircase. Bullet marks were clearly visible.

"Damn!" The inspector shook his head. "What the hell did he think was going to happen? Shoot you, then swan out of here unseen? Great plan."

"It can't be about the suspect. She wasn't even under arrest. Just taken in for questioning," Lerato leaned against the car behind her while the scratch wound on her temple was being treated.

Charlie rolled her eyes. "You think he wanted to scare us?"

"Good question." Marius walked up to the shooters and kicked him in the side. The man groaned. "Hey pologolo. What's your beef with these ladies here? Why did you shoot at them?" The security guard took his boot off the man's neck.

He stared at the inspector and babbled something unintelligible.

"He's Zulu," Lerato explained. "He's saying that he doesn't know what you are talking about." She let loose a barrage of words that Charlie assumed were in isiZulu and the man hurled obvious swearwords back at her.

"Ask him who Thomas is," Charlie suddenly said.

"What?" Lerato was slightly out of breath.

"Thomas. Ask him, who is Thomas?" Charlie repeated the name.

"Eish, you heard what she said," Lerato told him in isiZulu. "Who's this Thomas guy? Ungubani?"

The man grew pale, stared at Charlie and yelled "Umthakathi!"

"Bull's eye!" Lerato said with some measure of satisfaction. "He called you a witch. That means there definitely is a 'Thomas' involved." She let off another verbal avalanche that Charlie did not understand a word of.

"Khuluma iqiniso," Charlie suddenly told the shooter. "Scoundrel ezingcolile!"

She wasn't aware of the fact that she had just told him to tell the truth and called him a dirty scoundrel in isiZulu, but Lerato stared at her.

"Damn, girl I didn't know you could speak Zulu!" Lerato said.

"I can't." Charlie shrugged her shoulders. "I just told him to tell the truth."

"Okay… but you said it in isiZulu."

"Stop lying." Charlie giggled nervously. "That's not the time and place for jokes."

Lerato scoffed and repeated what Charlie had said. "Khuluma iqiniso!"

"Hamba kwalasha!" Go to hell. Two officers pulled him up by his wrists and led him away. He winced but tried to appear unaffected.

"I'm sure they'll sing now. Just look how scared he was of the witch," the inspector said and laughed abruptly. "To smuggle a gun into police headquarters and shooting it, is going to cost him dearly. What a stupid plan. My colleagues are going to teach him a lesson or two."

Charlie was shocked at the thought that the man would get hurt. "Is that really necessary?" Lerato looked away. So this was not unusual, then.

Charlie shook her head in disappointment. "I want nothing to do with that. This is my last case, I swear."

"I'll keep an eye on things," the inspector promised. "But if we want to find out the truth, this is sometimes what it takes."

"I feel like I need a shower." Charlie shuddered.

The medic finished treating Lerato's wound and fastened a bandage to her forehead. "I suggest, we go home now."

*

"That changes the situation considerably." Professor de Vries harrumphed.

Dr. Thokozo Sibanda sat next to him as they went

over the results of a forensic test the police had carried out on the blood sample. "Why would somebody do such a thing? Pig's blood!" He mumbled to himself.

"Maybe somebody tried to implicate Professor Morton's ex-wife on purpose or send a message of some sort," The inspector suggested.

"Like the mafia with a horse's head, you mean?" He answered.

"I wouldn't be surprised after the shooting yesterday."

The incident at the police headquarters had made the headlines, so everybody in the room was aware of what had gone down. Of course, the news had also highlighted the murder of Professor Morton and all that public attention was not helpful when it came to solving their case.

"Or maybe the pig's blood was part of some weird ritual?" Lerato put another idea forward. "Like an initiation."

They'd gone straight to Charlie's house after giving their witness statements. At that point, the document she'd found in Jeanne Ash-Morton's desk had no longer been a priority. Lerato needed to calm her boyfriend Peter down, who had insisted that she drop the case. Luckily, she'd convinced him with a white lie: that it was pure coincidence they had been near the scene of a shooting.

Charlie had also had her hands full with her brother Jono. She had begged him not to say anything to their family in New York. They were already worried about her and why make things even worse?

Both women had found their bearings after a few cups of chamomile tea. If anything, it spurred them on to solve the Morton case.

"Possible," Deon de Vries said. "But why did they soil Professor Morton's office? I cannot imagine that students could be so callous."

"Whoever did this must have been in possession of the key and knew that the blood would be detected sooner or later," Lerato said.

"Detection was obviously part of the plan." Inspector Vorster scribbled on his notepad. "As for the key… that's no obstacle, I'm afraid."

Charlie sighed. "First the murder in the Kruger Park, then the pig's blood in the victim's office and a shooting at the police HQ. How's all of this connected?"

"If anybody knows, it's you Ms Proudfoot - with your 'talent'." The inspector grinned, but nobody seemed to find it funny.

Charlie felt flustered by his remark. "What are you trying to say, Inspector Vorster? That's not how it works. I'm not an oracle. I sometimes get hunches, and most often, we apply a tried and tested technique called logical thinking."

The rebuke hit the mark and the inspector stopped grinning. However, he remembered all too clearly that Charlie had spoken isiZulu out of the blue.

Not at all what he had expected from the pretty brunette. It didn't take away from his attraction to Charlie, but he realised that making a joke about her talent had not been a good move.

"Sorry, I didn't mean to say it quite like that."

"Apology accepted." Charlie leaned back.

"Where does this leave us?" Dr. Sibanda sighed.

"The shooting could very likely be intimidation. You seem to be getting…"

Prudence, Professor de Vries's secretary walked in and waved for him to come outside. "What is it? We are in a meeting," he snapped at her.

"Somebody needs to speak to you urgently, sir," she said in a loud whisper.

The Dean grunted, "Excuse me, please," and walked out the door

It took not even five minutes before he reappeared and made an astonishing announcement. "I just spoke to one of our grad students, Irina Lotcombe..." They all recognised the name for various reasons. "She admitted to me that it had been her idea to spill the blood in Professor Morton's office last night. She's waiting next door for the inspector to make a statement."

Jaws dropped. The briefing took an unexpected turn.

"Now that's interesting news, and if it's true, at least one of our problems is solved," Lerato said. "I didn't take her for such a hot-head. Why on earth would she do such a thing?"

"She told me that Prof had gotten one of the students pregnant and forced the girl to have an abortion. If it's true, you have your motive at least for the pig's blood."

"I don't think that's true..." Charlie began.

De Vries interrupted her. "Irina says she was very angry about it. She knew the girl and was told after the research team came back from the Kruger Park. She never thought that Prof's ex-wife would become a suspect and is terribly sorry."

"Sorry? We questioned the woman for hours, yesterday." The inspector rolled his eyes. "Talk about wasting police resources!" He got up. "Let's not speculate. I'll speak to the student and see what else she has to say." He walked out and mumbled, "I can't believe this…" The door closed with a thud behind him.

"So there is no connection to our case?" Lerato was stunned.

"Let's give the inspector a chance. Although I must admit, that doesn't sound like Gerald," Dr. Sibanda said. "After the divorce maybe… but now?"

"Unless I'm missing something," the Dean backed him up. "Then again… I didn't know him too well. This should clear Jeanne's name, shouldn't it?"

"It doesn't explain the shooting, though, or the murder. We are still following several leads," Lerato declared to keep the conversation going. "We'll apply sound detective work and logical thinking as my associate here mentioned." She waved in Charlie's direction. "We'll update you on our results regarding the case. Would you like to add something?"

Charlie shook her head. "No, you said it all. I'm just not convinced that Irina Lotcombe is telling the truth. Perhaps we should wait for the inspector to come back?"

"It's his case and we need to get on with our leads," Lerato reminded her. "We can liaise with him later. It can take a while. I'm sure you gentlemen also have things to do?" The gentlemen nodded.

"Then I'd like to thank you for your time..." Lerato picked up her papers and the engraved silver pen she always clipped to her notepad.

"Wait a moment, please..." The professor cleared his throat and Lerato sat down.

"I feel terrible that we suspected Jeanne, but when I saw her making such a fuss about opening Gerald's office, I really thought..."

"We weren't present this morning, but to my mind, it's a perfectly acceptable assumption. We cannot strike her off our list of suspects just yet. As I mentioned, we are following several leads."

"I understand, but we have to, at least, issue an apology to her. I just hope we can resolve this whole matter quickly. Our fundraiser went very well, but it's getting more difficult by the day to convince the board that we should pay for the services of a detective agency."

"With all due respect, Professor," Lerato said sternly. "This is not a straight-forward case, and we still have to investigate if there is a connection to the shooting at the police headquarters. But if you'd rather just work with the police…"

"Certainly not!" Dr. Sibanda objected a little too quickly for the Dean's liking.

"Very well. I agree with you that the case is somewhat complex," he conceded. "Please do carry on with your investigations, Ms Gwala. And keep us posted."

"Thank you, sir. I can assure you… that's exactly what we'll do."

Charlie lifted her hand. "Can I ask you a question before we go? Does the name Thomas mean anything to you? Somebody with an interest in this case, perhaps?"

Lerato stared at her friend. Where did this come from?

"Not that I can think of," Professor de Vries answered and looked at his colleague. "Thokozo?"

"I know quite a few men, who go by the name of

Thomas. But no one that springs to mind. Please excuse me, I really have to go now. There's a trip to the Kruger Park to organise. We need to keep our donors happy or they'll leave without making good on their pledges."

"I'm sure you'll also want to see the killer of Gerald Morton caught," Charlie said.

"Yes, yes of course, and I have full confidence in your abilities. You seem to have things in hand."

"Indeed. Then we don't want to keep you. Have a good trip to the Kruger and good luck with the donors," Lerato said. "If you can think of anything … you know how to get in touch with us."

Chapter TEN

"How's your head doing?" Charlie was talking about Lerato's temple, where a shot had grazed her the day before. She had replaced the bandage with a plaster.

"Ah, it's only a scratch. Nothing to be worried about." The two sleuths were on their way to the cafeteria to discuss their case that was becoming more complex by the day. "It's more important that we find out, who this Thomas-guy is and what he wants from us."

"That's weird!" Charlie said as they walked down the passage past the office of the slain professor.

"What's weird? That the case is becoming more complex?" Lerato couldn't imagine what else Charlie was talking about. "Or that there is somebody called Thomas involved?"

"No that's not what I mean," Charlie Proudfoot scoffed. "I mean it's weird that snakes have lungs." She'd seen the picture of the green snake on the floor. Someone had placed it against the wall next to

Professor Morton's office. The glass was broken, but there were no shards, and presumably, the pig's blood behind the closed door had also been cleaned away. "So they do have cleaners here."

"What?" Lerato wasn't listening. "What lungs?" She looked up from her notes.

"Never mind," Charlie said. "At least we know now what the ghost tried to show me. What puzzles me is the connection to our case?"

"Maybe we're missing something."

"You can say that again," Charlie agreed.

She saw someone moving around a wooden bookcase further down the passage. The bright daylight streaming through a large window made it impossible to see the person properly. Could be a cleaner, she thought. It made the most sense.

"Wonder why they have cleaners and this place is still not clean."

"No idea what you are talking about, girl..." Lerato said absentmindedly and went back to studying the list of names from the Kruger Park. "Nobody called Thomas pops up here..."

"The sky is red and you have seven fingers on

each hand," Charlie sniggered.

"Really?"

"No Lerato, I'm just testing if you are listening to me and - you aren't."

"Sorry, doll, I'm going through my notes."

They reached the corner. A safari hat caught Charlie's attention and soon the whole spectre appeared. Lerato continued walking towards the stairs.

"Wait. Let's rather go straight," Charlie said and pointed to the bookcase. "That's not a cleaner after all."

"What? Who? Why do you even care?"

"I don't want to freak you out, but our ghost is back," Charlie said in a low voice.

Lerato looked startled.

"So you are listening now? Over there, by the cabinet."

"I can't see anything… just an old bookcase."

"And that surprises you?" Charlie walked a bit faster and Lerato tried to keep up with her friend.

"I don't know if I should be surprised or creeped out. What's he doing?"

"He's waving for me to come to him."

"That's so weird! What does he want? Be careful,

Charlie."

"You are here with me or not? The last time, he walked right through the door of his office and we found the blood there the next day. Maybe he wants to show me something important."

"I'm getting goosebumps. The stain was only animal blood and had nothing to do with our murder case… so how does that make sense?"

"Sshhh, we'll talk about it just now. He's saying something. Not sure what it is. The words are not clear and I'm not very good at lip-reading." She squinted at the ghost next to the glass cabinet only a few feet away.

"So what's he saying?" Lerato demanded to know.

Some students turned around and giggled. She ignored them and peered intently at the bookcase, still seeing nothing but a piece of furniture.

"He's pointing at a book on the second shelf from the top. Let's see…"

"He is? What book?"

"The one with the blue cover in the right corner. I think that's what he's trying to tell me. Look there…" Charlie stopped in front of the cabinet. The ghost nodded.

"What's the title of the book?"

"I don't know... let me try and open the sliding door. Damn, of course it's stuck!"

"Should we try and unstick it somehow?" Lerato asked.

"That takes too long. He's shaking his head and points to the wall."

"Goosebump alert. Is he close to us?"

"Umm, yeah."

Two boys looked them up and down. The ghost of Professor Morton pointed to the boys and proceeded to hit one of them – a ginger - over the head as far as that was possible for a ghost. He mouthed THOMAS.

Charlie turned and looked at the boy who grabbed his head. He had haughty, pale eyes and a shock of red hair that was tied into a fashionable high knot.

The other student touched his arm. "Everything okay, Tom?"

Charlie nudged Lerato and stepped towards the young men. "Excuse me... do you know Professor Gerald Morton?" She asked them and the look in their eyes was priceless. Their eyes flicked at the glass case.

"What? Why are you asking that?" The ginger snapped at her. He hadn't seen that question coming.

"We are detectives." Lerato showed him her ID. "We are working with the police on the professor's murder case. Just answer the question, please."

"Murder case? Well yes, he's one of our lecturers. Was... why do you want to know that?"

"Is your name Thomas?" Charlie cut in.

"Yes... Thomas Gerber. How do you know that? Why are you asking all these questions?" He looked more and more rattled.

"Your friend called you Tom."

"Oh... okay... but you... you have no right to interrogate me. I have done nothing wrong... and I know my rights. Leave us alone or I'll tell my uncle and he'll give you a piece of his mind."

"Easy tiger... nobody is interrogating you. Is your uncle's name Thomas as well by any chance?" Charlie asked him on a hunch and the ghost nodded seemingly pleased. The youngster seemed surprised.

"Yes, Thomas Bradwell. Why are you asking me that? Are you one of those mentalists, who can read minds?"

"What? No, I'm not a mentalist. We told you, it's about the murder case. We just ask routine questions.

If you want to get your uncle involved, be my guest. That means, you have something to hide and we'll find out anyway."

"You have no proof of that."

"Oh don't I? Let's say, I know that you have a headache. What else might I already know?" She winked at him for impact.

Thomas gawked in disbelief. "Come on Jimmy, let's get out of here. We must be at the tutorial in 5. They won't wait for us."

Professor Morton's ghost mouthed the word NESBITT.

"Jimmy Nesbitt?" Charlie asked.

"Yes," the other student said visibly startled. "We're running late because of these old ladies here."

"Hey, watch it, wena!" Lerato flared up at the obvious slight. "Umsunu wakho!"

"Ha? An old lady with a dirty mouth!" Jimmy cried and pulled Thomas by his elbow, staring anxiously back at the detectives as they hurried around the corner.

"I think we freaked those two out," Lerato chuckled.

"There's something about them. At least we have

their names and obviously, they have something to hide," Charlie said. "The ghost told me to speak to this red-haired boy called Thomas."

"He did? How did you know about his headache?" Lerato touched the plaster on her forehead. She knew the feeling.

"I saw the ghost of Professor Morton knock him on the head."

"What? Can ghosts do that?"

"Apparently."

"Hmm, good for him. Cheeky buggers: leave us alone or I'll tell my uncle …" She said in a mocking tone. "Pathetic little maggot. What does your ghost have to say to that?"

Charlie looked up. The ghost was gone! "I don't know. I can't see him anymore."

"Damn! Your ghost is elusive." Lerato knitted her eyebrows. "Is he expecting us to thumb-suck the connection to his murder?

"I'm sure we'll figure it out. We already know more than we did five minutes ago." Charlie was crouching next to the bookcase. "And by the way, he's not MY ghost…"

"Alright, THE ghost then. I think I know why the boys were so scared."

"You do?"

"Remember the document I found in our lady-professor's desk?" Lerato asked.

"Yes, you still haven't told me what that was all about."

"Too much going on... but there is a possible connection. Time to have another look at that document. Let's go to the cafeteria and I'll show you."

"What about the book?" Charlie asked.

"What book?"

"The one in the blue cover on the shelf over there."

"Oh yes, right. The one the ghost showed you..." Lerato said.

"Exactly. It could be evidence. We'll have a look at the document, and then we'll find out what's so important about the blue book. Killing two birds with one stone - so to speak."

"Well, let's see what we've got here. How are we going to explain to our detective that we suddenly found that book?"

"We could say that somebody told us to look there.

We don't have to say, who showed it to us. Some student - forgot the name."

"Okay, that's simple enough. We could do that, I suppose. Politicians forget facts all the time when they are questioned. So we can forget a name…" Lerato tried to push the glass door open again. It didn't budge. "Damn it's stuck for good. Any more force and the glass will break."

"Wait, why don't we try to open it from the back? The ghost pointed to the wall, didn't he?"

"If you say so. But we better don't cause damage to property…"

"Ah, fiddlesticks! Help me push the case forward," Charlie Proudfoot was unruffled.

The ghost had shown her the blue book and she'd be damned if she didn't try and find out what this book was all about.

Lerato put their bags on a nearby chair. "I think just this side will be fine. But Fiddlesticks? Your South African heritage is shining through." She giggled.

"I guess so. Okay… 1, 2, 3…"

The two women pushed against the cabinet and it slid forward easily. It was obvious that the back had been opened before. A number of staples were missing from the thin Masonite backing, and the top corner flapped back when it was no longer supported by the wall.

"Well, I'll be damned!" Lerato whistled through her teeth. "A secret post box?"

A student walked past and gave them a dirty look.

"What's a secret post box?" Charlie wanted to know.

"You leave secret messages there… hmm, looks like your ghost has a point." Lerato pulled the backing to the side and fumbled for the blue book. She pulled out a yellow one first. The cover fell open and revealed pages that were cut out to form a square hollow. There was nothing inside.

"Wow. It is a secret post box alright. I wonder what for."

"It's not the book we want," Charlie reminded her.

"Pity," Lerato said put the yellow book back. "This was starting to intrigue me. She pulled out the blue book and they read the title together: Mugwort, Wormwood, Sagebrush, A Complete Study of Zulu Medicinal Plants, University Press, by H.O. Peppctta, W. Hurwitz, T. E. Shabalala et al on the front of the dust cover. The photograph of a bushy plant was on the back. Silvery leaves and little yellow flowers that crowded the tip of the branches. It didn't look exactly remarkable.

"Okay, no surprises here. That's undoubtedly academic, but not very zoological."

"No, it's the wrong faculty." Charlie stared at the book, trying to make sense of the unforeseen riddle.

"Hey, what do we have here? A bloody fingerprint! At least that's what I think is." Lerato showed Charlie a brownish stain on the back picture.

"I think you're right. What's a book on plants doing here?" Charlie stared at the fingerprint on the blue dust cover.

"It looks like a thumbprint," Lerato mused and turned the book slightly. "So somebody took the book, got blood on it somehow and put it on the shelf in the wrong department… must have known about the open back of the bookcase…"

"Shouldn't you be using gloves or something?" Charlie asked.

"Damn, you're right. How could I forget? Do you have a tissue? Never thought we'd find that kind of evidence today when we're not even looking."

"I have some tissues in my bag. Just drop the book in my lap for now."

"Okay… and tissues coming up…" Lerato took out the paper tissues from Charlie's bag.

"You can put it in my snack bag. Take out the sachet with the sunflower seeds and the apple. The plastic bag is big enough for the book."

"You and your Mary Poppins bag." Lerato winked at her. "Sunflower seeds with barbeque flavour - interesting. By the way, isn't it time for you to eat proper food? Since we are on our way to the cafeteria anyway..."

"Yes, Mom…" Charlie laughed and got up from the floor.

"Okay then, let's do some brainstorming over lunch. I can't wait to show you the document I found in the lady-professor's desk."

As soon as they'd arrived at the cafeteria, they bought some food and started their meeting, forgetting about the noise around them.

"If this is what I think it is… then it's bad news."

Charlie put Lerato's cell phone back on the table

and shook her head. "How can she be so corrupt? Imagine these graduates let loose on society…"

Charlie was talking about the document Lerato had photographed on the night of the donor-event. There was no doubt about it: Jeanne Ash-Morton, a distinguished professor of botany was involved in a scheme where 'service providers' sat exams, wrote essays and dissertations for students with the necessary cash. It cost 15,000 to 120,000 Rand depending on the service offered.

The document showed names and fees neatly listed in spreadsheet rows and columns. One of the customers was a certain Eugene Gerber, and there was another familiar surname… Elsabé Nesbitt.

"Our lady has a network going – parents are willing to pay big bucks for this and our Prof takes her cut. A nice little side gig." Charlie shook her head and drank from her water bottle.

"And now we know why our boy Thomas Gerber looked like he'd seen a ghost. No pun intended." Lerato chuckled.

"Yip, underachievers with oodles of money pay poor but smart suckers to write their essays for them, their dissertations and what not." Lerato sipped on her coffee.

"It's not unusual to go online and find so-called providers. In America at least. Been going on for years. Have you never watched the series Suits?"

"Actually, no. How out of the loop am I?!"

"No seriously. It is all about paying somebody to write a paper. The student presents the paper as his/her own work, and the act of writing it isn't even illegal. Using it and pretending that you wrote it yourself, that's where the waters become murky. I know of a couple of students who were caught stealing the work of other students online and got suspended." Charlie nibbled on the remains of her Greek salad.

"No way! Why did I study on my own steam, then?"

"You are an honest person, like most people, and you don't have that kind of money. Is it unfair? Sure it is, but there will always be cheaters and hangers-on and they usually trip up somewhere. Call it karma."

"Karma… hmm. But being caught at cheating is hardly enough motive for murder." Lerato didn't sound convinced. "Did Gerald Morton threaten to expose her?"

"I doubt it. That would have called the new project

into question."

"So, what does your intuition say?"

Charlie pondered the question for a moment. "That you are probably right. There must be another motive behind Morton's murder. And why did Irina Lotcombe draw attention to his office with the pig's blood? That also doesn't sit right with me."

"As a distraction? Irina now claims that Pericles Duncey told her about the alleged affair and abortion."

"So she's throwing Duncey under the bus? I don't get it. Why would he tell us about the evidence of a cheating scandal in Jeanne Ash-Morton's desk?"

"To implicate her? He doesn't seem to need the money, but he knows about the scheme." Lerato nibbled on her lunch.

"You mean he wanted to distract from himself... and then attract attention?"

"Let's look at the facts: our botanist was nowhere near the Kruger Park, and I can't see her hiring thugs to carry out the killing and shoot at us. There's just not enough motive. She wasn't even a suspect until she tried to stop the police from searching the victim's office," Charlie said and tackled her salad again.

"Then we'll have to find the motive. It has to do with the blue book. I'm sure of it."

"Which takes us back to the virus-busting plant project and the investors. Just where does the bloody fingerprint come in?"

"Maybe your ghost can shed some light on it?" Lerato suggested.

"I told you – he's not MY ghost and I can't exactly talk to him. Hang on… Morton's office is in the Zoology Department. They pour blood on the floor to make a point. The motive is iffy, but the shoe prints roughly lead to the back of the office, then to the glass cabinet… didn't they?"

"You mean that the blue book was in Morton's office. Irina took it and hid it on the shelf? Then our grad student is not as innocent as she pretends to be, just trying to avenge her friend…"

"Or Duncey made her do it," Charlie suggested. "For some other reason."

"Or that."

Girls at the table next to theirs started laughing uproariously and two of them chased each other for a portion of slap chips.

"Here, you need to eat your mini-pies. I got you the crust-less ones." Lerato pushed the little carton with the pies towards Charlie.

"Thanks. I keep forgetting to eat when I'm busy. Actually, my blood sugar is more normal now. The doctor told me to keep doing what it is I'm doing."

"That's wonderful, Charlie. Can you reverse the diabetes?"

"Doctor Els says that it's not diabetes yet. More to do with the stress of grief than anything else."

"Well, then you have to eat properly. Here, eat your pie or must I feed you?" Lerato took one of the pies and made Charlie take a bite.

Charlie chewed obediently. "This is good," she mumbled with her mouth full of pie.

"It's legendary." Lerato smiled and finished her coffee. "Back to our case, fellow detective! We need to make a list. Testing the fingerprint, questioning suspects..."

Charlie took another bite from her mini-pie. "I think there's an indirect connection to the cheating scheme. And a direct one to the shooting yesterday."

"That means we need to establish a link. Florence

can do some research for us and Marius Vorster might also have an idea or two."

"Did you tell him about your little excursion into Jeanne Ash-Morton's office?"

"No. Maybe I shouldn't even try."

"Then, we can hardly discuss the Thomases with him. Or the blue book. And we have to tell him about that."

"Remember our anonymous informant?" Charlie prepared to eat the second mini-pie. "It wouldn't even be a lie. But the way he acted during the meeting today... oh God... we are stuffed. He can't know about the ghost."

"Okay, forget about the police for a moment," Lerato said. "Let's move on to our lead here. All we need is the dust cover for the lab. They will check out the fingerprints quicker than the police."

"Let's see why the ghost wants us to look at this book." Charlie slipped the blue dust cover off and opened the book. "A bookmark - now that's handy! There are probably fingerprints on the bookmark as well." She put the bookmark carefully into the plastic bag.

"Let's see: Agrotora, species Artemisia afra, Daisy family Asteraceae, Higher Classification Anthemideae... daisies. What's that all about? Daisies?" Lerato was amazed. "Flowers?"

Charlie pondered this. "I keep thinking that it could have something to do with the project Pericles Duncey and god-knows-who are invested in. But then, all we have to do is find out at the patent office. So why hide this book?" She bit into her pie.

Lerato googled on her phone. "Let's see what this Agrotora plant is good for: grows in the wild on damp slopes alongside streams and forest margins… blah blah… a condiment with supposed magical properties… hmm… to treat bronchitis, coughs, colds, fever, loss of appetite, headache, colic… antiviral properties, painkilling, relaxing."

Lerato nudged Charlie's arm. "Antiviral properties! So it's true. A treatment for HIV perhaps? I'm thinking this could be the same tea my gogo made us when we had a cold."

"Your granny made you guys tea from this plant?"

"Bitter as hell."

"Hmm… apparently it's also used in poultices, infusions and Wilde-als brandy – whatever that is - to name a few. Traditionally also known as wormwood, it has a very bitter taste and is usually sweetened with sugar or honey…"

Lerato picked up the book and studied the page. "It's not exactly rare… so what's so special about this plant?" She put the book down.

"It must be working against a very specific kind of virus to be so special. HIV is a good guess. There's also this research on new types of viruses. I'll look into it."

"Could be something to it." Lerato closed the book and placed it in the bag. "The fingerprint is my department. We might just find out, who tried to hide the book."

"What's my department, then? Scientific research?"

"Exactly – and ghosts, of course," Lerato said. "Okay, you ready? Let's go."

Charlie shoved the last bit of the mini-pie into her mouth. "Ready."

"We should go to my office. You haven't been there yet and I must introduce you to Andy… oh wait, he's probably with his wife and the new baby. But we could speak to Florence. She's a star when it comes to online research. "

"That sounds good." Charlie placed their trays on the

conveyor belt by the kitchen before leaving the cafeteria.

"I knew you would come in handy," Lerato giggled.

"Gee thanks, girlfriend. Glad to be of service."

They were on the way to the car when Lerato noticed Jeanne Ash-Morton walking past them with a surly-looking man. "Isn't that the ex-wife with William Brewster, the American tycoon?"

Charlie turned half-way and saw them from the corner of her eye. "Look at that! I wonder what he is still doing here. Aren't the donors supposed to be on their way to the Kruger Park?"

"A billionaire can go whenever he likes. He'll probably join the others later."

Chapter ELEVEN

The office of the *Maitirelo P I Agency* was on the first floor of a modest building in Parktown North.

Charlie and Lerato were greeted by a pretty young woman at the reception desk that several businesses shared. Phone calls were routed to the switchboard and answered by two secretaries.

Florence and Ayanda were students, who took shifts during office hours. The PI agency paid Florence, a part-time marketing student, an additional salary to assist with cases. Andy Malherbe had installed specialised software on a laptop that was locked away when it wasn't her shift.

Andy was Lerato's business partner and like her, a retired police officer. He was currently on paternity leave, so Florence was a godsend. Thankfully, it was a quiet day at the switchboard.

"Hi Flo, this is our consultant and my friend Charlie Proudfoot," Lerato introduced the women.

"So you are the famous Florence," Charlie greeted the

receptionist.

"Nice to meet you. Oh, I didn't know that I was famous already," Florence chuckled. "Lerato, I got the patent search result for you. Lodged by - guess who - Kannemeyer, Bradwell & Associates, patents attorneys. THE Mr. Bradwell. Wait…and here are your messages." She opened a drawer and took out a few pink slips. She had also learned from a contact at the police headquarters that the arrested shooter was still in interrogation.

"Thank you, Flo. Now that's interesting. Mr. Thomas Bradwell is an attorney." Lerato looked over the short print-out. "As expected… pharmaceutical patent for traditional medicines, herbal product inventions. Unlikely, that they will get the utility patent for our mysterious Agrotora plant, though. It's just too common."

"What's a utility patent?" Charlie asked.

"Oh, if you create a plant and want intellectual property rights for your invention. So it's more likely that the pharmaceutical patent for traditional phytomedicines will go through. Once they have the South African National Standard, they can apply for a worldwide patent. Or perhaps, they already have. Lots of money in that, too." She handed the documents to Charlie.

"Florence, could you please look into that law firm – the patents lawyers – find out if they have links to the names Duncey and Brewster? Especially in the US - anything that could link them to our case. Oh yes, and please look up info on these new viruses. Perhaps there is already a link to the compounds mentioned in the patent… Charlie will evaluate the search results. She's a biologist."

Lerato gave the receptionist a list Charlie had prepared. "Oh, and I need new business cards. Could you order 100 from that place down the road?"

"I'll get right onto it. Just give me an hour or so." Florence took notes while she answered an incoming call. "Hold on, please." She pushed a flashing button on her switchboard.

" Lerato, I nearly forgot. The lab phoned about the tyre tracks. They found some pollen and a squashed flower on the cast. I'll forward the report to you."

"Thanks, Flo. We'll touch base later."

Florence nodded and turned her attention back to the caller.

"That's a neat arrangement you have with her," Charlie said as they walked up the stairs to the Maitirelo office. "And look at that brass sign on the door: Maitirelo Private Investigators. Impressive."

They entered and Lerato threw her keys onto the filing cabinet next to the door.

"I wish I could afford her full-time. Flo's reliable and a fast learner, too. Handles computers better than I do. She had no issues with signing the non-disclosure agreement and hit the ground running."

"Maybe one day you'll be able to employ her."

"Maybe." Lerato checked her phone messages. "Mr. Hammond again… he wants extra surveillance, but he still needs to pay us…"

"Can I have a glass of water, please?" Charlie asked.

"Sure. Clean glasses are next to the kettle and water comes out of the tap."

Lerato switched on the lights in an adjoining room and Charlie followed her with a glass of water. A large wooden table took up most of the space. It had done duty in Andy Malherbe's kitchen before he got married.

She put the blue book cover on the table, then photographed the thumbprint and took the cover and bookmark to the reception. "Florence will arrange for it to be picked up by the laboratory driver."

"Okay, I'll just sit here and think." Charlie tried to connect with Gerald Morton's spirit. She wanted to ask him to help put the puzzle pieces together. But there was no connection at all.

"The Mortons have been busy," Lerato said when she returned with more print-outs. "Florence found something about the ex-wife's paper on the 'Efficacy of the Alcoholic Extract of the Agrotora Plant'. A clinical trial shows that it could be used in combatting virus infections. Specifically lung infections."

Charlie roused herself from her dreamy state.

Ping. "Ah, the report from the lab." Lerato opened the file on her cell phone. "Okay, the cast Sergeant Mokhodi took. The lighter soil found closer to Hoedspruit. Then, there was pollen and a flower from the flame tree stuck to the cast. Found in the timeshare complex. Okay, that's not proof but narrows it down. That means that at least one of the holiday makers was at the crime scene. According to the lab, the flower was still fairly fresh. Only lighter soil on the cast that I took. That was a bit of a fail. But definitely a Hilux."

"That's something," Charlie said.

"I'll send this report to the inspector. He can give our people in Hoedspruit a call."

Charlie was studying the pages that Florence had printed out. "Bingo, here's a study on corona viruses. Looks legit, although nobody else is taking them seriously at this stage."

"Why isn't it taken seriously?" Lerato wanted to know.

"There are hundreds of them and not well studied. Often carried by animals," Charlie said. "It says here that on occasion they can jump to humans and cause disease. So far just cold or flu symptoms. Only two cause serious disease in humans: SARS and MERS, but in 2004 the SARS virus disappeared. The Middle East Respiratory Syndrome was identified in 2012 and there are only small, local outbreaks. Nobody thinks that they'll be high risk anytime soon."

"Then why go through all that trouble of getting a patent for the extract? What about HIV?"

"Apparently, no connection to HIV. It says here that Agrotora was tested on SARS and the results look promising. In case of another outbreak, an effective product is ready for treatment. There could be a market in the future as a flu remedy or such. That should be worth a bundle."

"Alright then," Lerato put the book inside the filing cabinet. "It doesn't sound like it's worth all that effort. We already have flu injections."

"Gerald Morton thought that there might be a virus epidemic sometime in the future," Charlie said. "I watched a pandemic doccie on Netflix, but who knows…"

"So they did research based on his vision of a future epidemic? Expensive exercise." Lerato looked bewildered.

"According to the study, it's only a question of time before this type of virus becomes a serious problem. It just seems that nobody is sharing his vision just yet." Charlie turned the page. "Apart from an institute in Antananarivo. They have a similar plant that's indigenous to Madagascar, and Morton was about to sign a contract with them a week ago. To do more research."

"Hmm, sounds a little *pie-in-the-sky* to me. If nobody, except an obscure institute in Madagascar wants to research this, why is it important?" Lerato asked.

"I don't know, but something tells me that we should dig deeper."

"If you say so, Ms Geneticist. The ghost also seems to take it seriously – if he's not playing games with us..."

"He seemed to take it very seriously when he showed me the book. I still feel we have overlooked something. Why they have such bigshot investors for one thing."

Lerato's cell phone rang. 'Oh okay, sorry. I'll be there in 10,' she said and hung up. "Damn it's hard to be professional when you're in love."

"Why, what is it?"

"It's Peter. I forgot our lunch date in Rosebank. Can you drop me off at the Rakers, please? You can have my car to drive home. We'll pop around to your place later to pick it up. I should have some more news by then."

"That gives me some time to think. Intuition likes peace and quiet. Where are your car keys?"

Lerato looked around. "Here." She picked them up from the top of the filing cabinet. "Alright girl, you give it some thought while I have lunch with my boyfriend."

A message came through on her cell phone. "The lab

says they'll fast-forward the test. The blood test is relatively simple. I'll pick up the result after lunch. The lab is just around the corner from the Rakers Restaurant. Peter can take me there. "

"Deal," Charlie said and they left the office.

*

When Charlie Proudfoot pulled up on the driveway, a white car was parked outside in the shade of the large hibiscus. She didn't pay much attention to the vehicle and drove in and parked behind her own car. Clearly, Jono was not at home.

She walked into the kitchen and the dogs were overjoyed to see her. Charlie made herself a cup of tea and took the print-outs to the lounge.

Billie and Popcorn settled on the couch and she turned on some music.

"Speak to me," she said aloud and sipped on her tea. "What's behind all of this? Wild dogs, an unwanted pregnancy, a wonder cure for viruses? Big money and the ex-wife... a bloody fingerprint on the blue book. Come on, help me out here... how does it all fit together?"

Her cell phone played the title melody of the movie

'Out of Africa' and Charlie's heart missed a beat. "That was quick…"

To her surprise, it was Inspector Marius Vorster. He told her that she shouldn't be alarmed in case there was a car parked outside her house.

'Why, what's this about?'

'We have been questioning the hitman, who shot at you,' the inspector said.

'Yes, and what did he say?'

'Not just him. Irina Lotcombe gave us some important information, but I can't give you all the details now. Please do me a favour and just stay at home.'

'That sounds ominous. Are you saying somebody is trying to hurt me?'

'In a manner of speaking… not just you. I can't get hold of Lerato. Is she with you?' Marius Vorster sounded worried.

'In a manner of speaking? What's that supposed to mean?'

'I'll tell you later. Is Lerato with you or not?'

'She's not. Lerato is on a date with her boyfriend at the Rakers Restaurant in Rosebank. She probably switched her phone off. But, inspector, you have to give me something, here…'

'Well… the shooter says he was supposed to send you a warning for you. To get off the case. He just didn't get away quickly enough.'

'What on earth?' Charlie hollered. "He could have done some serious harm."

'Remember that you asked him about someone called Thomas?'

'Yes…'

'It turns out that Thomas Bradwell, a lawyer, paid him.'

'Okay, no surprises there. We've already come across the name.'

'We need more evidence to make it stick.'

'Yes, of course. Lerato wanted to look into this Mr. Bradwell and his law firm's connection to Duncey and Brewster. We ran into Bradwell's nephew at university and he behaved… a bit strange.'

'A bit strange?'

'He threatened us with his uncle if we asked him questions. And we just asked if he knew Professor Morton. And somebody told us to look for a blue book in the passage of the Zoology Department. So we did.'

'Yes?'

'We think it might have something to do with the pig's blood incident and the Mortons' project. There was another book on the same shelf…'

'I'm sorry, but can this wait? We must get hold of Ms Gwala as soon as possible. We can touch base later.'

'What did Irina say?'

'That Pericles Duncey told her about the girl with the abortion. We are still trying to get hold of the woman to verify Irina's story.'

'Hmm… so the volunteer and benefactor of the department tells Irina about this and not the wronged girl herself?'

'Okay, let's talk about this later. We need to find Ms Gwala. Do me a favour and don't leave the house until we can be certain that you are not in danger.'

'Danger? What danger?' Charlie exclaimed.

'No time, I'll explain later. Oh, and if Pericles Duncey phones you, let us know.'

Click. The dogs looked at Charlie with big eyes as her phone rang again almost immediately.

'Ms Proudfoot?' A haughty male voice asked.

'Yes? Speaking.'

'It's Pericles Duncey. Would you be able to come to the university? I'd like to talk to you and Ms Gwala about something.'

Charlie wanted to hang up but thought better of it. 'Oh right…yes… where would you like us to meet?'

'Shall we say in front of the cafeteria at half-past two?'

'Very well, we can meet there. Bye for now.' Click. She wondered what that was all about and why he suddenly wanted to meet with them. There was something the police knew about this man that she didn't.

She heard a noise by the kitchen door and the dogs sat up growling.

"Jono, is that you?" she called. "Jono?"

She heard heavy footsteps. A man entered the lounge and the dogs were barking wildly. Charlie jumped up from the floor, where she had been sitting.

"Who the hell are you and how did you get in here?"

*

Three smartly dressed patrons, who could have passed for lecturers, sat at one of the shady stone tables outside the cafeteria. They were having a conversation amid the hustle and bustle of lunchtime at the university. Well, one of them was a lecturer. The others not so much, yet something profound connected all four of them. Greed.

Thomas Bradwell, Jeanne Ash-Morton and William Brewster were waiting for Pericles Duncey. They were here to discuss serious business. Duncey was running late for their ad hoc meeting, but that wasn't unusual.

William Brewster's valet sat on a bench closer to the cafeteria entrance and watched the students file past him. Noon was the busiest time and he needed to be careful not to lose sight of his boss.

Lerato Gwala and Peter Munirwa sat at one of the stone tables by the tower. They had moved their lunch date from Rosebank to the university on a whim because Lerato wanted to see Irina Lotcombe, who was still busy in the library.

To her surprise, the student had phoned to say she wanted to talk. So Lerato would sneak in some questions for Irina while being on a date with Peter.

'You don't mind, do you love?' She'd said.

Peter had not been happy about the change of location. 'I've already ordered a drink,' he feebly objected at the Rakers Restaurant. "And I'm hungry."

"We can get something at the cafeteria," she'd beamed at him.

Of course, he did mind. This was not the romantic lunch date he had in mind, and there was another reason why he would've rather stayed in Rosebank. A rather important reason.

But when he saw how eager Lerato was to speak to the student, he had no longer objected. Although Peter knew he would regret it.

Traffic on Jan Smuts Avenue was light and they arrived at the university in no time. "I can't stay too long. We have a virtual meeting at about three," he told her.

"It's fine if you have to go. I can speak to Irina alone." Lerato looked around. "I'll just wait here."

"At the cafeteria? No… it's okay, I'll stay with you. Why don't we just wait by the library and eat some takeaway there?"

"How lucky is that?" She whispered.

Her trained eye spotted Mrs. Ash-Morton in an elegant outfit. She sat at a table with William Brewster and some other guy in a suit.

"What's lucky?" Peter asked in an uneasy tone.

"Can you believe it? A few of our suspects are sitting together, chatting. Odd place for a highfalutin meeting… or smart. And there is Mr. Duncey… what do you know..."

She took a photograph with her cell phone, pretending to pose for a selfie.

"Oh man… " Peter mumbled. He recognised the American tycoon and cast an unhappy look at Brewster's valet, who guarded him. *Good, they haven't seen us yet... there's still time to act.*

"Let's go inside, darling." Peter tried to sound calm.

"No, why?"

"It's getting a bit hot in the sun."

"I like it out here. I can't let an opportunity like that slip through my fingers…"

Lerato tried to pick up snippets of the conversation.

"We should start without him," Thomas Bradwell suggested. He hadn't seen Duncey walking towards them. "Peri's always late."

He put his reading glasses down a little too forcefully. His brown eyes almost disappeared in the burly face. Thomas Bradwell was a stocky man and the expensive suit he was wearing didn't temper his appearance one bit.

"I have another meeting in an hour and that client won't wait. Jeanne and I must discuss another matter as well." He turned to the professor. "Do you want to do this now? I have the envelope..." Mrs. Ash-Morton shook her head slightly and shot him a warning glance.

"Let's start, Tom. My helicopter is on standby. Going to the Kruger before... you know..." William Brewster was interrupted by the late arrival.

"I'm sorry... traffic." Pericles Duncey had been directed to the meeting by Brewster's valet with a nod of his head. He let himself fall onto the empty chair and the meeting began without delay.

"So the patent is going through soon if I understand Jeanne correctly," William Brewster bellowed and the professor put her hand on his arm. "Lower your voice, Will." The billionaire smiled an apology.

"Alright, alright," he said in a softer voice. "I'm used to addressing a boardroom full of managers. So, as you already know, we are helping the process along as much as we can. Now it's time to start developing the merchandise."

"When?" Thomas Bradwell asked.

"Next week or so. Now that we have a quasi-timeline, we can get on with it. I've told my marketing people to come up with a concept just as we discussed. They already have a few names for us. NoFlu48, ColdBeGone and NeverFlu."

"Do we decide on the brand name now?" Pericles Duncey asked peevishly.

"No we don't, but it would speed things up."

"Okay then, NeverFlu is catchy. What do you guys think?" Jeanne Ash-Morton said. They quickly settled on a name for the new flu medication and Thomas Bradwell took minutes.

"That was painless. If we can agree on everything else so quickly, we'll be out of here in no time." Brewster grinned.

"Here's to hoping," Bradwell said tetchily. "I don't know why we had to meet here."

"Let's not go into that again..." Jeanne Ash-Morton sighed.

"Okay, let's get to the less pleasant item on the

agenda: finances," the tycoon continued unperturbed. "I'll foot the upfront marketing costs, of course. We'll calculate it into the final agreement, but we need to get a running start. Jeanne will take over Gerald's share. It seems, they had an arrangement and he updated his will the week before the expedition to the Kruger Park."

He leaned back and stretched out his legs. "Dang uncomfortable chair."

"What? How does that make sense?" Pericles Duncey was clearly not in agreement with something. Lerato wished she could be close enough to hear what was being said. Her lip-reading skills were not very good. She took another picture.

"Let's go inside, Lerato, you've got what we came for. Those pictures are plenty of proof that they had a meeting."

"Why are you in such a rush, Peter?" Lerato asked absentmindedly.

"I'm hungry."

"We can get takeaways and eat in the car after I speak to the student…"

"Maybe we should go now. Can't you send the

student a message that you'll speak to her later?"

"Peter, it's important that I stay here. Go and get something to eat if you must, or drive back to the office."

"Well, then… I tried." What did they expect him to do? He could hardly wrestle Lerato and drag her to the car-park.

"Wait, it's getting really interesting now. They are arguing," she said.

"You can't even hear what they're saying." Peter became rather nervous and looked at the valet from the corner of his eye. Lerato was too engrossed in what she saw to pay much attention to her boyfriend.

Pericles Duncey seemed rather agitated.

"We all made… made this happen," he hissed and his eyes darted around to make sure nobody else had heard him. "All of us agreed to it and we should all get a share. I took a great risk… you know that."

"Look man, nobody said you should go that far," his American cousin said.

"So it's all on me now. Are you serious? And I'm not even benefitting?"

There was an uncomfortable pause that would have been worse without the background noise. The traffic on the highway, chit chat and laughter and blaring music from cell phones. Eventually, William Brewster harrumphed and tried to speak as calmly as possible.

"As long as we all stick to our story, we'll be okay. They are groping in the dark and things will blow over before you know it. We have to concentrate on matters at hand if we want to make this work, now that Gerald and his silly ideas are out of the way. So thank you, Pericles for taking the initiative, but don't expect an award."

"This has nothing to do with the consortium and each of us will make enough money to retire comfortably. Oh wait… you are already retired," Jeanne Ash-Morton said sharply. "Pull yourself together, Pericles. We have business to discuss."

"Business as usual, hey?" Pericles Duncey breathed in deeply. "And act as if nothing happened? That's too much to ask."

"Now kids… let's not argue. We are all relieved that our main problem has been solved. I say that if they had an arrangement and the will was changed, then that's what goes." Thomas Bradwell said. "As much as I would like a higher cut myself, a legal arrangement is a legal arrangement."

"Do you even know what it feels like? I've been going through hell since… since... We must all benefit from the new situation. The things I have done, I did for the consortium - for all of us!"

"Benefit? What do you mean?" William Brewster bristled. He had no stomach for his second cousin's blathering. The boy was getting out of hand. "That was the whole idea, wasn't it? To smoothen things out, so we all benefit – for once."

Pericles and his mother had already benefitted greatly from his brother John's will. What more did he want?

"Remember who came with you? Who flew out to the Kruger to meet you, support you? Because you couldn't do it alone? My foot! All the things you've done for the consortium…" Thomas Bradwell began to feel flustered.

"Here's the thing, in case you've all forgotten: we couldn't persuade Gerald to develop the flu medication straight away. He was never one for large profits," Jeanne Ash-Morton flared up. "His beloved conservation projects were priority number one. And no… he wanted to develop some far-fetched remedy against virus infections that might or might not cause an epidemic somewhere, sometime in the future."

"To help humanity," William Brewster snorted. "For the record… I didn't even know about your plan."

"He just wouldn't listen to reason," the professor continued. "Do you think it was easy for me? He was my… husband… at some stage at least, and I did love him… then. But what choice did we have?"

Thomas Bradwell nodded. None of this would go into the minutes, of course.

"Let's not even speak about your hare-brained idea with the pig's blood. You couldn't discuss it at least with me? Your little stunt had the opposite effect and got me almost arrested." She tried to keep her voice under control.

"As if Tom's idea to send some incompetent gunman into the police HQ was any better!" Duncey protested.

"Big M has never let me down before, but he better keep his mouth shut."

"You guys are some mobsters. I hope you're not doing anything else so stupid. Pericles, I'm talking to you." William Brewster looked sternly at his cousin.

"Get off it, Will. You have no idea how things work around here."

"Look, let's not fight over this," Bradwell said firmly." We'll never get this project off the ground if we start to turn on each other. Then nobody will benefit. I'll tell Janine to get the documents ready asap… we can sign when you're back from the Kruger, Will. Then we'll move on."

The aggrieved Pericles Duncey murmured his objection, but the majority ruled in favour of the existing agreement and Jeanne Ash-Morton was satisfied with the outcome.

Duncey was in a bad mood when he spotted someone he was expecting to meet, and his mood lifted instantly. Good, he thought maliciously. Now, where was the other PI? He took out his cell phone and dialled a familiar number.

Lerato took another picture of the clandestine meeting, pretending to be a selfie queen. The burly-looking guy whispered something into the professor's ear and handed her a thick envelope.

"Well I'll be damned. I bet this is Thomas. They are leaving now… I wonder what exactly their discussion was about," she said to Peter.

"My guess is money and how to get more of it by any means possible. Why would people like that meet here? They have all the fancy boardrooms in the world and then they come here to meet on campus."

"That's exactly what I was thinking, but they are harder to trace here. In case they were under observation. Should we follow them?"

"I'm hungry, remember? And I must get back to the office now."

"So let's get our takeaway food - something quick. It's almost 2:30. I hope Irina's on time. I'll make it up to you, I promise… we must…" Lerato stood up and Mr. Brewster's valet bumped into her.

Her cell phone fell to the ground. "Hey, can't you be more careful?"

"Sorry about that. Wait let me…" The valet bent down and picked up the phone. He gave it to Lerato and gawked at her. "Haven't we met somewhere?" He asked.

Lerato started to giggle. "That's a cheesy pickup line if I ever heard one. No, we haven't met. Hope my phone's okay." She switched it on, trying to shield the screen from Mr. Brewster's valet. "Yep, still working."

"Rick, what are you doing over there? Flirting with the girls on the job? We must go. The helicopter is waiting."

"Sorry sir, I'm coming."

In passing, Rick saw Pericles Duncey grinning like a Cheshire cat and there was nothing he could do.

Chapter TWELVE

Charlie stared at the badge the man was holding up and began to comprehend.

"Sergeant Dlamini, madam. We are your detail outside - in the car. Could you please…" he pointed to the dogs.

"Oh… you gave me a fright, sergeant. Billie, Popcorn, shush! Come here, come here." Charlie tried to calm the dogs. They stopped barking at high-pitch and huddled by her feet. The policeman put his badge away and looked at the door.

"Sorry to frighten you, but this man tried to enter your property with a key. We picked him up outside the gate. He says he's your brother, but clearly, he's not. Could you please confirm this, so we can take him into custody?"

Jono walked into the lounge with the other policeman. He was holding Jono by the elbow and her brother glowered at him, shaking his hand off. The two dogs sniffed at the men and danced around Jono making happy noises. The policemen stared in surprise at the unanticipated reaction.

"I told you I live here. Charlie, tell them who I am. That's the second time in as many weeks that I've been taken for an intruder." He rolled his eyes and bent down to pet the dogs.

The policemen looked confused.

"Sergeant Dlamini. Thank you for looking out for me, but this really is my brother. We are adopted siblings and we live together on the property." Charlie Proudfoot exhaled sharply. "And if he was a real intruder, why would you just bring him into the house like that? What if he was planning to harm me?"

"Oh… sorry, ma'am. Sir… Mr. Proudfoot?"

"Morake."

"Mr. Morake. We didn't receive a briefing... there was no time. We just wanted to clarify... but of course…" the sergeant stuttered. "Sarel, come on let's go back to the car. Our apologies again. We'll be outside if you need us."

"Could you wait a second, sergeant?"

"Ma'am?" Sergeant Dlamini turned around.

"Inspector Vorster wanted me to tell you when I

hear from Pericles Duncey. Well, he just phoned me."

"Right, he's one of the suspects…what did he say to you?"

"He wants to meet with me and Lerato Gwala at the university. The entrance to the cafeteria at 2:30. Could you please tell the inspector about this?"

"I'll certainly let him know. We'll take care of it."

"Thank you," Charlie said. "Could you tell him now? It seemed urgent."

"I sure will."

The sergeant took out his phone and followed his colleague into the passage.

"Goodbye, officers. Please remember my face…" Jono said in a mocking tone.

"Sorry again, sir. It was our mistake."

The two policemen left, but Jono didn't look any happier than he had when they'd entered the room.

"What the hell is going on? Can't I come home without being accosted by strangers? Why has Marius put a detail on you in the first place?"

"I'm not sure, something to do with the case. I just spoke to him, and he explained that there's a police car outside. They want to make sure I wasn't in danger. He didn't have time to explain. So I don't know much more than you do. I'm not supposed to leave the house and they are also trying to find Lerato in Rosebank."

"What's she doing in Rosebank?" Jono asked.

"Meeting Peter for lunch at Rakers. We went to her office then I gave her a lift to Rosebank. She said I should take the car. Peter and Lerato will come by later to pick the car up. I'm worried, Jono. She's not answering her phone."

"Umm, okay." Jono looked confused. "That explains why her car is here." He sat down and the dogs jumped on his lap. "Easy, Popcorn. Yuck, don't lick my face," he laughed. "Okay, let me get this straight. He thinks that you and Lerato are in danger and that's why you have security outside?"

"Well, something along those lines. I hope Marius has found Lerato and that she's safe. The police got a lead through the guy who fired at us… and Irina, the student also gave him some information."

"That's good news, isn't it?"

"Well, it's not so good if somebody is trying to kill us."

"No, of course not." Jono took a deep breath.

"First the shooting and now this. You must be getting close to the truth."

"The inspector didn't have time to give me the skinny on it, but I guess you're right. Damn, I wish there was something I could do. He also told me to let him know when Pericles Duncey gets in touch."

"I heard that. Did you try to phone Lerato yourself?"

"Not yet, but I can try." Charlie dialled her friend's number and a recording came up: the subscriber is not available at present, please try again later. "She must have switched her phone off."

"Try Peter's number," Jono suggested.

"Damn, I don't have his number. Do you?"

"I think so... yes, here it is... Let me try on my phone. That's quicker... 5754... It's ringing... yes, hi Peter, it's Jono, Charlie's brother."

He began a longwinded explanation, so Charlie took the phone from him. 'Put Lerato on, Peter. Let me explain it to her.'

'She's not here, Charlie. She said she'd do some research in the library. What's all the fuss about?'

'What were you doing at the university – and why is

she not answering her phone?' Charlie wanted to know.

'Long story and she can't answer her phone at the library. Let her explain it to you when she gets a chance.'

'Which library, Peter?'

'Yes, dinner sounds good. Give Billie my best.' He hung up.

Lerato's eyes were wild with despair as she cowered on the tiled floor. She couldn't speak because of the duct tape that was stuck over her mouth. Her attempt to make a sound and warn Charlie was cut short. The guy who was guarding them slapped her and Lerato went limp.

'Why do you have to hurt her?' Peter reproached him angrily. 'Leave her alone.'

Her hands were tied to her back, but Peter was free. She had tried to fend the two thugs off, who'd waylaid them on their way to the library. Pericles Duncey had waved to them from afar, grinning.

Peter sat down protectively between his girlfriend and the brute with the gun and gently tried to wake her up. The unpleasant smell in the men's room, a mixture of urine and disinfectant, should have done the trick all by itself.

All he could do was keep his wits about him. He'd done his best trying to keep Lerato away from the university, but she'd been attracted to this place like a moth to the flame. Had she listened to him, they wouldn't be here now, afraid for their lives. It had all started yesterday in his company's underground parking.

Mr. Brewster's valet had approached him and asked for his help with some car problem. Of course, they had never met. He must be here on business, he'd thought. Wrong.

'Look, I don't know much about cars, but I'll try...' he had said good-naturedly and regretted his helpful gesture almost immediately. The man had suddenly pushed him against a black Lexus and shoved him into the car without an explanation. Some other guy in a suit was already waiting for him on the backseat. 'Mr. Munirwa... did I pronounce that right?' Also an American.

Peter nodded silently, suddenly afraid. Who was this guy and what did he want from him? Rich - obviously. Peter was dealing with rich businessmen all day long.

'How kind of you to join me. I believe we haven't

met, although your girlfriend is an acquaintance if you can call it that. Right now she's sticking her nose where it doesn't belong and that is getting in the way of my business.' The rich guy drawled in a broad accent. Peter now recognised his face from an online article on plastic pollution he'd recently read. What was his name again..?

'I'm not going to explain the whole story to you because then I'd have to kill you… haha ha… a joke.'

Peter stared at him in disbelief. Isn't that what people said in bad movies?

'Here's what I want you to do: take your girlfriend to a restaurant for lunch tomorrow. Far from the university, and keep her there until – let's say – 3 o'clock. Easy enough, right?'

'Why?' Peter didn't understand.

'Never mind that. Let's say it's in the interest of her health. Understood?'

'No, I don't understand. What do you want with us?'

'That's for me to know and for you to find out. …'

'Right. Can I go now?' Peter couldn't wait to get out of this car and this potentially unsafe situation with the American mobsters.

'Just a little warning before you go: nobody is to know about this. And I mean nobody or your girlfriend will pay for it. And believe me when I say… I'll find out.'

To Peter's surprise, they had let him go and he'd walked over to his Opel. The Lexus zoomed past him and left the underground parking. A note was stuck to his windscreen. It read: Nobody!

His hands trembled all the way back to his flat. Peter was so distracted that he scraped along the kerb when he turned into the complex.

He tried to get his head around the fact that he'd just received a warning from what felt like the Mob to him. What did one do in a situation like that? He was only a chartered accountant, not James Bond! After a glass of red wine to steady his nerves, he was finally able to phone Lerato.

'The Rakers in Rosebank?' She sounded surprised. 'That's different. We're busy with the case, but I'm sure I can get away for an hour or so. Okay, let's have lunch for a change. I didn't mean to neglect you, but this case is taking up a lot of my time. Everything alright with you?'

"Of course. I can't wait to see you, darling.' Peter tried to speak in a normal voice, but his thoughts were still racing long after he'd hung up. All he had to do was keep Lerato away from campus until after 3 o'clock and they would be safe. It was clear to him by now that all of this was connected to the case Lerato was working.

He found the article about plastic pollution on Google News. The mobster's name was William Brewster, an American billionaire connected to the Republican party. It didn't paint a rosy picture of the man's character and shady business dealings.

Peter still felt bad for not telling Lerato at the time. He'd wanted to protect her, but maybe things would have taken another turn if he had.

He placed Lerato's head on his thigh and checked her breathing. She was alive.

The men's bathroom was in a hidden corner of the building. Nobody had been around when Duncey's thugs had taken them there through a back door on the lower level. The guard had locked the door from the inside and hung an "Under Repair" sign up outside. The whole thing must have been planned. Nobody would come here to look for them.

Peter knew he had to stay calm if he wanted to buy them time. This situation was his fault. He had failed to protect Lerato by not telling her the truth.

"Don't worry. If I wanted her dead, she'd be by now." The guard opened the door a crack and peeked outside. He nodded to the other guard by the stairs, then quickly locked the door again and washed his hands in one of the basins.

"Darn, only cold water and no soap."

"It's a university, not a hotel," Peter said and was pleased to see that this smug guy had to wipe his hands on his smart trousers.

He was still angry with himself that he hadn't anticipated the ambush. It had taken only a minute in a narrow service lane. Then the heavies had brought them here to the men's toilet without saying a word.

Brewster left by helicopter with his lackey to join the other donors in the Kruger Park. Strangely, Pericles Duncey seemed to be in charge here and not the mobster tycoon. Why had he tried to warn Peter to keep Lerato away? So those two toffs were connected, but pulled in opposite directions?

Lerato's boyfriend tried to get his head around it. She moaned a little.

"Why do you have to be so brutal?" Peter flared up again.

"She shouldn't be snooping around... Some people don't like that sort of thing."

A wave of guilt washed over Peter. "That's still no reason to hurt a woman."

He felt the broken cell phone pieces in his pocket. The man had stomped on Lerato's phone during the scuffle and he'd managed to pick some of them up. Jono might be able to retrieve the pictures later. Later...

"The other one had the sense to stay away. Scared by being shot at, I think. Sometimes it works, sometimes it doesn't." The guard guffawed.

"You mean Charlie?"

"I think so. Duncey phoned some chick while we were watching you and told her to come. It would have been two for one, he said. Thought they'd come together."

He pointed his gun playfully at the ceiling.

"Do you always do everything you're told?"

"It's my job and I don't get caught like Big M. The

lawyer and Duncey are badass, but they pay well."

"Why are you telling me all this?" Peter wanted to know.

"It doesn't matter. Soon, you won't tell anyone anymore…"

I wouldn't be too sure about that, Peter thought. He could feel Lerato coming to. She moved a little and he took her hand. "Take at least the duct tape off her, so she can breathe."

"Nah, she'll try and scream again."

"Nobody will hear us here and anyway… she's no fool."

"Alright then. You can do it."

Peter ripped the tape off Lerato's face and she grunted without waking up.

He stuffed his jacket under her head, unrolled some toilet paper and wet it in the sink. Why doesn't she wake up? He thought while gently dabbing her forehead.

"If you have money and power, you call the shots. That's just how it is," the thug offered his opinion and pointed his gun at the mirrors. "Brewster is Duncey's cousin. It's all in the family."

Peter nervously watched him handling the gun. "So Duncey's rich, hey?" He turned his attention back to Lerato. Maybe the guard would be kinder if he kept talking to him.

"Richer than Thomas. Look, the guy's a jerk and his mother, well… you're getting the picture. But they pay me well. As long as I do as they say, I'll keep my job."

"Who is Thomas? I thought Brewster's name is William."

"Look, you're talking too much, man. I don't have to explain anything to you. It's just what it is."

Peter was still busy dabbing Lerato's forehead with the cool, moist paper.

"What are you going to do with us?" Peter knew he needed to make a plan. Any plan before it was too late.

*

"That was strange," Charlie gave the phone back to Jono.

"What was strange? Don't you believe Peter?"

"I'm not sure, but why would he say 'dinner sounds good, give Billie my best'? Why would he say that? Dinner? And he knows that Billie is a dog."

"Weird."

"He tried to warn me. Maybe they've already got to Lerato - and Peter's there with her. Marius didn't find them in time…"

"Oh boy." Jono tried to think. "We have to let the inspector know."

Charlie was already on her phone and explained that Peter had obviously tried to warn her about something.

'Wait, wait, wait. I got your message about Duncey's phone call. Sergeant Dlamini told me a minute ago. Lerato is not at the restaurant in Rosebank, then?'

'I'm pretty sure they are at the university somewhere.'

'But where? Do you have a hunch?'

'More than a hunch. He kept saying that she's at the library."

"Hang on… there is a phone call coming in. It's Irina Lotcombe." The inspector sounded surprised. "Let me quickly take this."

*

It went down in a flash. The guard outside the secluded men's room under the stairs was swiftly overpowered. Then, on a silent count to three, officers in bullet-proof vests forced the door open. The OUT OF ORDER sign flew all the way to the staircase as they stormed inside.

Marius Vorster, who led the police operation, guided out a stunned guard in handcuffs while paramedics attended to Lerato and her boyfriend. She was still dazed, but her head injury was luckily superficial. Peter had suffered a cut on his hand during a brief scuffle and the ensuing rescue.

"Thank God... how did you find us?" Lerato asked, freed from the duct tape. "Did you find Duncey and the others?"

"Not yet. Irina Lotcombe alerted us. She phoned me to say that you were going to meet her at the library. She saw two guys drag you and somebody else away. That's when she realised that something fishy was going on. Your associate, Charlie Proudfoot, phoned me two minutes later and said she'd spoken to your boyfriend. That you were at the university and not in Rosebank. She knew something was off."

"Yeah, she's good. They were all in a meeting outside the cafeteria."

Lerato told the inspector what she had witnessed. "And I still don't know why Irina wanted to see me."

"To come clean on her affair with Alan du Plessis, the ranger. Duncey caught them on a tryst and blackmailed them."

Lerato stared at Marius Vorster. "Are you serious?"

"Yes, that's what she'd told me before. Duncey told them what to do. That's why we didn't know that Bradwell had been to the Kruger Park and that's why she helped Duncey with the pig's blood and took the book to the shelf in the passage."

"Duncey was behind that all along?"

"Not just that. According to Irina, he'd lost his marbles after that day in the Kruger. He'd told her about Prof. Morton's affair that resulted in an abortion. She was angry, but when she asked around, nobody knew about it, and Sarah, the allegedly wronged woman thought Irina was positively mad for even suggesting it."

"So he was going mad? But what about Prof. Morton's murder?"

"We'll talk about it tomorrow at the HQ. The ambulance will take you to the clinic for observation.

It's procedure, just in case."

"First the shooting," Lerato said and touched the plaster on her forehead," and now I get myself roughed up. Not my finest performance."

"I heard there were some incidents before…"

"Are you saying I'm accident prone?"

"Not at all. I mean you didn't get hurt."

Johan Phaladi called Inspector Vorster over. He'd just heard how Lerato's boyfriend had been approached by William Brewster and his sidekick in the parking garage the day before.

"Wait…" Marius Vorster stopped him. "Why would Brewster warn you to keep Lerato away from the university cafeteria if he was planning to shut up the PIs?" Marius Vorster asked.

"Maybe Brewster is the better person. To be honest, I think Duncey and Brewster can't agree on anything. They are relatives but don't seem to like each other very much. I'm told that it was Duncey, who did this to us."

"I see," Marius Vorster said, "So why did you come to the cafeteria when Brewster warned you?"

"I had every intention not to come, but Lerato can

be so stubborn. She just didn't want to stay in the restaurant. When the student phoned, she arranged a meeting, but we had to wait for her. When Lerato saw all these suit-people having a meeting, she decided to wait outside the cafeteria. I couldn't get her to come with me. Why didn't she listen to me?"

"You should have contacted us. You had goddamn luck, Peter," Inspector Phaladi scolded him.

"Who came to the meeting?" Inspector Vorster asked him. He wanted to cross-check the facts, Lerato had already given him.

"I saw the woman-professor, I think, William Brewster, the lawyer-guy, and Duncey came late. Brewster's lackey was also there."

"By lawyer-guy you mean Thomas Bradwell? The man, who organised the shooting at the SAPS headquarters?"

"I think so. I don't know these people. Lerato told me who's who in the zoo. So you should ask her."

"We'll do that. How's your hand?" Marius Vorster asked him.

"I'll live. It's more important that my girlfriend's alright. I'm so thirsty."

Inspector Phaladi handed Peter a bottle of water. He greedily chugged the water and glanced at Lerato who sat on the stairs, surrounded by paramedics.

"Where are they taking her?" He saw them leading her away.

"Just to the clinic for observation."

*

The police in Hoedspruit took William Brewster, the untouchable tycoon, into custody as soon as his private helicopter landed in the Kruger Park. Alan du Plessis, the ranger Irina Lotcombe had named as the other witness on the afternoon of the fateful day in the Kruger Park was called in for questioning.

At first, he refused to cooperate. He was a married man after all. But before long, he verified what his lover had already told the police: that Thomas Bradwell had picked up the volunteer, Pericles Duncey, not far from the researchers' camp in a Toyota Hilux.

Alan had agreed to keep silent or his wife would find out about his tryst with the student. He also was to make sure that Bradwell's name didn't show up on the list of people, who had stayed at the timeshare complex, and took the lawyer's name off the list of pilots, who had landed on the nearby airstrip.

"Bradwell told me that the murder weapon was in the small lake behind the trees. A fire extinguisher. You know a small one for the car."

"Alan, I can't tell you how disappointed I am in you," Sergeant Mokhodi said. They were in the small but tidy police station in Hoedspruit. "How long have we known each other? 10, 15 years?"

The ranger hung his head in shame. "Liesl would have found out, and what about the children? This Bradwell guy and Duncey meant business. I've never seen this popinjay act so mean."

"Your wife is going to find out now anyway and you very nearly helped the killers get away with their crime, Mr. du Plessis." Inspector Vorster and Lerato Gwala looked at each other.

They had travelled to Hoedspruit to wrap up the homicide investigations. There had been a series of arrests in Johannesburg, and even though William Brewster had connections in high places and hired a capable law firm, he remained under house arrest at his hotel in Sandton.

The high-profile murder case was coming to an end and the press showed great interest given the international relations between South Africa and the US.

As to the motive of the murder, it turned out that it had not been straight-forward greed.

The perpetrators and the victim had known each other since their high school days. Pericles Duncey had a crush on the blonde girl for as long as he could remember, but she hadn't even seen him.

The gawky teenager made moon-eyes at the beautiful science nerd. He knew that he was out of her league when it came to understanding maths and science. But there was hope that she would come around if he wooed her the old-fashioned way. Expensive gifts, restaurants and outings.

His overbearing mother had encouraged his efforts because Jeanne was from a well-to-do family. Alas, Jeanne kept saying that there was just no spark. Then, just as he'd worked up his courage in their matric year, Gerald Morton had come along and those two had hit it off immediately.

Duncey was convinced that Jeanne was his soulmate and Gerald Morton had taken away any chance of their happiness. Nevertheless, he volunteered for research projects that he'd supported with good money to stay close to them.

When their marriage didn't work out, Jeanne had not even considered Pericles a worthy rebound lover after the divorce. Instead, Thomas Bradwell showed an interest in the attractive botanist and was found to be worthy.

He'd saved himself for her all these years and Thomas was married. The insult hit deep. Thomas and Jeanne had been lovers for two years and started a successful cheating scheme as a side hustle, but serious business was much more profitable. Well, Duncey had put paid to that.

When Gerald Morton mentioned scientific findings regarding the antiviral properties of the Agrotora plant, a new business venture was born. Duncey had made sure that he was on the consortium.

His cousin, William Brewster, had signalled interest and offered to market the product in a hundred ways and a romance with Jeanne kept him sufficiently interested in the project.

"Women can be so fickle," Pericles Duncey said in

a bitter tone.

Thomas Bradwell's motive had been less about passion but business. An inconvenient obstacle had to be removed. The chess pieces started moving as soon as the expedition took Prof. Morton out of town.

They all knew about the denning and Pericles Duncey had kept in touch with him. Timing was everything. Although he hadn't wielded the fire extinguisher, he had aided Duncey in every other way he could.

"We didn't plan on doing it that way. With the fire extinguisher. Pericles saw Gerald sitting there and grabbed it as he got out of the car. We hadn't really thought it through…"

The cheating scheme was just part of the game of money. His brother had become a prominent plastic surgeon, but a dumpy 34-year old woman wrote the thesis in his stead for a princely sum.

"It was too cumbersome for him, so the family had to organise a loan. His nephew was going the same route, but now the family was swimming in cash."

And why not? His brother wrote it off as extra tuition fees.

"Gerald knew nothing about levelling up. He's always been at the top. The plant project was about business. Bloody do-gooder didn't understand that. What can you expect of a man who dedicates himself to the ugliest animal in Africa?"

Charlie shook her head. She was following the interrogations behind a one-way mirror in the room next door. Lerato was good at this.

Next up was Jeanne Ash-Morton. Inspector Phaladi left the room and Marius Vorster took his place.

"I tried to change his mind, but there was no reasoning with Gerald. He insisted that a future corona epidemic was on its way," the woman rolled her eyes.

"Imagine that," Inspector Vorster said. "Did you know that he'd received a letter that a German laboratory offered to come on board with the promise of substantial funding?"

"No, I didn't know that." The professor seemed astonished. "How much funding?"

"It doesn't matter now, does it? Professor Morton wrote in his notes that he was beyond thrilled." The inspector read. "'As if the birth of a litter of healthy wild dog pups and the progress with Madagascar wasn't exciting enough, the Germans have agreed to give us money for research.' He wanted to share the good news with the consortium after his return from the Kruger Park."

"Blast it," she said in an unlady-like manner and her attorney put a calming hand on her arm. But there was no stopping Jeanne Ash-Morton now.

"Pericles Duncey and his mother bought out Nivedna Naidoo, the tetchy veterinarian. She wanted to extend her surgery and needed money. When she learned about the anticipated profits, their sneaky move rankled with her. It made business sense to get her out, but Nivedna hated us for it," Jeanne Ash-Morton complained to Lerato and the inspector.

"Why kill your husband, then? You could have talked him out of his plans."

"He was stubborn. The project was supposed to make us wealthy. Imagine - a new effective flu remedy. William told us that 'it would fly off the shelves'."

There was a bitter tone in her voice.

"Of course, everybody would want to make a buck. Times are tough," Lerato said.

The policewoman by the door changed her weight to the other foot.

"You can say that again," the professor snorted with contempt. "That old fool didn't care about the money. The tests would have taken years to complete."

"That's simply too long if you can make money now."

"Damn right. Nivedna gave Pericles a hard time and he was thinking of rubbing her out as well. Actually, it was his mother's idea, but the others were dead against it... would have caused too much of a stir. We just waiting for the patent to come through. William gave Thomas money to grease palms... then 'World here we come!'" They watched her face contort as she recalled the events.

"How wonderful that would have been. You had a lot riding on this."

Her attorney cautioned the professor not to divulge too much information and she gave him a stern look.

"Yes... time is money," she mused, then changed her tack. "You mustn't think that it was just about the money for me. Gerald didn't even care about William and I. Or Thomas! How cold is that?" She seemed stricken by her ex-husband's lack of interest.

Charlie shook her head behind the one-way mirror.

"She wanted to make him jealous?" Inspector Phaladi said in disbelief. "They weren't even married anymore."

"It couldn't have been love for her," Charlie said. "Attention maybe? But then… hell hath no fury like a woman scorned…"

*

"Thomas Bradwell, you say?" Deon de Vries, the head of the Zoology Department, took the news calmly. He had done his job and management would lavish praise on him.

Possibly even a seat on the board. The only problem was that the department had to fill the positions of a zoologist and a botanist. But he already had his eye on some acquaintances.

"Yes, not only was he involved in the murder of Gerald Morton but also ran a cheating scheme with his ex-wife. We've handed our evidence over to the police."

"Very well, thank you for all your efforts. I'll arrange for the balance of your payment to be loaded, Ms Gwala. You should have the money by the end of the week. Well done. If you'll excuse me now, I'm expected at a press conference."

Lerato, Charlie and Inspector Vorster nodded. They had just finished their debriefing session with him. The professor left his jacket on the chair and Prudence, his secretary came in to collect it.

"Thank you so much for solving the case," she said and wiped away a tear. "We will miss Professor Morton around here." She left the room sniffling.

"That's exactly the impression I'm getting," Charlie said.

"It seems they got a cheating scheme into the bargain," the inspector pondered. "That should give de Vries major brownie points with management."

To Charlie and Lerato it felt good to win a victory for justice against all the odds.

*

"I can't believe the professor's ex-wife was angry that he wasn't jealous of her lovers. Look how she was carrying on."

"She was angry enough to kill him off. Then our Duncey-guy hated him because he was jealous. And all of them saw Morton as an obstacle to becoming even richer. You can't win. That's why a good guy had to die and our new cure for the flu might never see the light of day." Lerato put a large helping of potato salad on her plate. "Hmm, I love your potato salad, Charlie."

"Wait for the boerewors, it's nearly ready." Jono moved the large sausage spiral to the side of the braai grid where the glowing embers had already cooled down.

"There is plenty of space for boerewors where the potato salad is going," Lerato chuckled. "Beer anybody?"

"Naw, Just Coke Zero for me," Charlie said. Lerato topped up her glass.

"All three of them arrested for murder and accessory to murder. Pity though that William Brewster's lawyers got him off the hook so quickly. I hear he's back in Texas. I still can't get my head around this consortium and what they did. How evil can you be?" Peter said.

He was today's braai-master and set the tongs to the lamb cutlets. "Also almost done. Perfect. Jono, hand me the dish over there, please."

He was still quietly recovering from the shocking

abduction he and Lerato had gone through only three weeks ago.

"You'd be surprised. But it all worked out in the end. Their glorious consortium fell apart when they turned against each other."

"But, that a brilliant guy had to die because of some corrupt morons. Poor wild dogs have lost a champion and what if an epidemic really does happen in the future?" Charlie said.

"Girl, I can't think anymore. It's been a stressful couple of months." Lerato still had a thin scar on her forehead, thanks to the grazing shot she had sustained at the Police HQ in town.

"You won't need my help with the next case. It will be straight forward and you won't get winged by some stupid hitman. Easy peasy."

"Easy peasy? Is that a prophecy?" Lerato mocked Charlie.

"Didn't you say it was easy peasy for me to solve cases?"

"Yeah, I guess I did. Remember how your ghostly friend came through for us?"

"He didn't actually say anything when he

appeared, but he certainly did help us." Charlie laughed. "Well done, Gerald!"

The others lifted their drinks and toasted the ghost of Prof. Gerald Morton.

"I hope he rests in peace now and that somebody is taking up his cause with the African wild dogs," Jono said.

"Oops, I think we're out of ice for my killer Gin & Tonic." Peter lifted the empty ice bucket. "Can you take over for a moment, Jono?" He handed him the braai tongs.

"Aye, aye sir."

Charlie patted her friend's arm. "How are things with Peter?" She whispered.

"We'll see. It wasn't his fault that they jumped him at his workplace, but he should've said something to me. I could have stopped the whole thing."

"He'll learn. Give him a chance. Peter's a real nice guy."

Peter came back with the ice and mixed his famous sugar-free G & T and they all toasted to the successful completion of the Morton murder case.

"Follow the money…" Peter lifted his glass.

"Well, money can't buy you love."

"At last, we agree on that."

"Okay people, let's sit down. The boerewors and the lamb are ready."

"Smells delicious."

"Who's up for some boerewors?" Jono asked and cut the grilled sausage into pieces. Billie and Popcorn danced around his legs, begging for scraps.

They laughed and tucked into the food.

"Hey you two, don't trip me up," Jono scolded them. "So Lerato, what are you working on at the moment?"

"I can't talk about specifics, but it's nowhere near as exciting as the last case Charlie and I worked on. Stake-outs mostly, jealous husbands and stuff like that. My partner Andy will take over from me when Peter and I go on holiday."

"You know what it's like with a new baby. They've been basically hibernating, but now I need a break."

"So you'll be missing the ceremony the Biology Department organised to scatter Professor Morton's ashes at Emmarentia Dam? Jono and I are going."

"Yeah no, we'll be in Port St. Francis on that

weekend," Peter said and cast a loving look at Lerato, who enjoyed a bite of boerewors.

After dinner, they sat around the fire pit as the sun was setting. "I love the fire. It's hypnotising to look into the flames," Peter mused.

"Isn't it just?" Lerato sighed.

The dogs had settled on top of Charlie's feet. "Look at our wild dogs."

Jono's cell phone rang. 'Don't you answer the landline anymore?' His mother asked. 'We've been trying to phone you.'

'Sorry, mom. We're outside, having a braai.'

'That's nice, Jono. Getting into the South African spirit again?'

'Yes. We invited a couple of friends over. You remember Lerato?' Charlie walked up to her brother and listened in to the conversation.

'Of course, I do. Charlie is working with her on murder cases. I don't like the idea of it… neither does your father, but as long as you two are alright.'

'Yes, we're fine, mom,' Jono replied. 'What's up in New York?'

They heard their father talk in the background.

'I'll get to it, Itu," Mrs. Morake fussed. "So, your Dad and I have been talking. Term break's coming up and we thought that, since we miss you so much… well, that we should book a holiday in the Kruger Park and stay with you in Joburg for a few days. What do you guys think?"

The End

THE AUTHOR

Evadeen Brickwood grew up with two sisters in Germany and studied cultural sciences and languages. As a young woman, she travelled extensively and many of her books are inspired by her experiences abroad. Feeling adventurous, the newly qualified translator moved to Africa in 1988 and worked for two years as a secretary and language teacher in Botswana. The author eventually settled in South Africa, where she got married and raised two daughters.

In Johannesburg, Evadeen Brickwood studied computers and management of training and worked as a corporate software trainer, professional translator and lecturer at WITS University. In 2003, she began her writing career with youth novels in the 'Remember the Future' series, about adventures in prehistory. Book 1, the award-winning 'Children of the Moon', has been published twice in South Africa and translated into German. The author now self-publishes and you can look forward to the new, off-beat Charlie Proudfoot series, which is set in South Africa.

The author's websites are:

http://www.evadeen.wixsite.com/charlieproudfoot

http://www.evadeen.wixsite.com/novels

http://www.evadeen.wixsite.com/youngbooks

Evadeen is looking forward to your mail and can also be contacted on social media, incl. Facebook, Twitter, Instagram, Pinterest, google+ and Goodreads.

ABOUT THIS EPISODE

When my mystery novel „The Rhino Whisperer" was released in 2017, my distributor in South Africa told me how mad he was about wildlife and could I please write a book about the endangered African wild dog. This has remained at the back of my mind ever since.

When the Charlie Proudfoot series came together, I decided to honour his request and let African wild dogs make an appearance in one of the episodes.

That's why the storyline in „Claws Out" takes us to the Kruger Park, where much of the conservation effort is taking place. The university I mention is a construct of my imagination, although I must admit that there are similarities to the university in Johannesburg where I lectured for many years.

My research into wild dog conservation has renewed my utmost respect for the many rangers, scientists and volunteers, who so selflessly work at protecting our priceless wildlife in Africa.

Although the story is entirely fictional, I hope that I managed to capture the unique feel of the African bush we all enjoy so much.

Evadeen Brickwood

THE NEXT EPISODE
in the Charlie Proudfoot Series

3

A young woman from a wealthy family is found
hanging from a tree in a popular Johannesburg park.
Her death causes a public outcry. Not only is it the third
suspected femicide in a month, but Candace Sedibe was
also pregnant. What role does the owner of the online
dating website SugarDaddyDateMe play?
Then our two sleuths discover that there can be a dark side
to the glamorous sugar baby lifestyle.

https://www.amazon.com/dp/B08PS56YWZ

MORE BOOKS BY EVADEEN BRICKWOOD

This adventure mystery tells the story of 22-year-old Bridget Reinhold who is not exactly the adventurous type, but when her sister Claire disappears in Southern Africa, nothing can hold her in England. Bridget launches herself into the search in Botswana and encounters obstacle after obstacle. She learns the basics of the native language and culture and soon moves to the capital city of Gaborone. Soon, her mission is plunged into turmoil as everything seems to be going wrong. Just coincidence or is there something more sinister at work?

Another mystery novel set in modern South Africa. This time, the murders of a ranger and a rare black rhino in the idyllic Shangari Safari Park rattle the local community of Rutgersdrift. Sofia Helenius from Finland lives at the lodge with her boyfriend Tom Rutgers, the owner of Shangari. Sofia is tormented by a secret she yearns to share with Tom, but the cruel events grab the limelight and put everything else in the shade. One of the native Khoi-San families is known to communicate with wild animals, but what if the criminals get wind of this gift?

When another murder happens in the city of Johannesburg, smouldering secrets begin to unravel. How are the murders connected and will it be possible to halt a relentless crime-syndicate in order to save an African paradise?

As if growing up in the seventies wasn't difficult enough, teenager Isabell Bertrand is also too rebellious for her parents' liking. A novel treatment with hypnosis appears to be the perfect remedy and Dr. Albrecht regresses Isabell to her early childhood and even further back. She experiences previous lifetimes and then one in particular: could this beautiful young woman in a silk sari, who was forced to choose between two men, really once have been her? Years later, Isabell is invited to a wedding in Pakistan and memories of a forgotten love come flooding back - with dangerous consequences.

Can you imagine, suddenly living in the past? Not last year or in the Roman Empire, but a really, really long time ago?

Katherine, Trevor and Chryséis embark on a sea voyage and sail across the prehistoric ocean to the remnants of a sunken continent. Suddenly everybody seems to be after a mysterious speaking stone from the fabled land of Lyonesse.

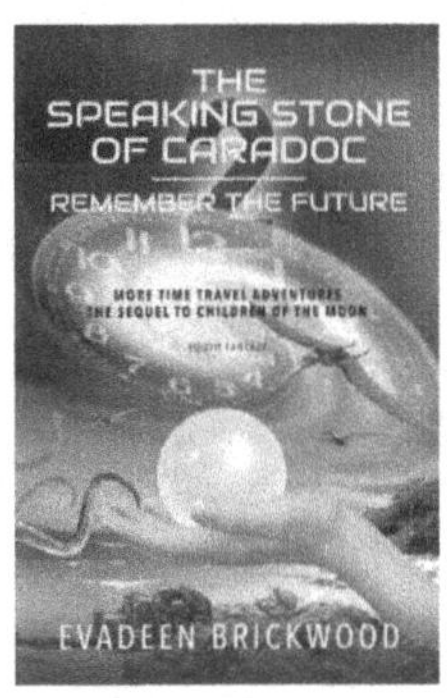

Finding their way back to Alesia and their home in the future, turns out to be more difficult than the time travellers thought. War breaks out in the Mediterranean Sea and forces Katherine, Trevor and Chryséis to flee inland. Nothing here is the way they thought it would be, and who has ever heard of Egypt without pyramids?